MW01268659

FAKE DATING HER YETI

ALASKA YETI SERIES
BOOK 2

NEVA POST

ICICLE INK, LLC

Created with Vellum

A yeti boss that's too hot to be true.

Toni, a smart and successful business owner from Alaska, never envisioned herself in a fake relationship—until her mother's nagging takes its toll. She could appease her mother and help her friend and boss by agreeing to be his plus one at a looming Thanksgiving wedding. But she risks more than just her business reputation, she risks her heart, too.

A crush on an off-limits employee.

What could be worse than watching your human half-brother get married to your ex? Being single and furry when they tie the knot. Denzin is the regional manager of a busy guiding service company, so he knows better than to date an employee, even if it is pretend. But when their deception turns into something real, it might be Toni who ends up breaking his heart.

CHAPTER ONE

> Toni: Your tux is here. Custom made to fit a yeti. *smiley winky face*

Denzin scowled at his computer screen. His annoyance had nothing to do with the message and everything to do with what the tuxedo represented.

Rejection. Inadequacy. Loneliness.

He had to get over it. This weekend, and his human half-brother's wedding, would pass soon enough.

Before he responded, another message popped up.

> Toni: Also, Eddie is here. Early staff meeting? Dress code optional, the boss in a tux won't intimidate us.

The corners of Denzin's mouth lifted at Toni's teasing. A part of him wanted her to see him in his formalwear before the wedding and gauge her reaction. Would she like what she saw? He hoped so. But that train of thought wasn't at all appropriate. And he'd never act on such impulses, no matter how much he longed to. At least not since he'd hired Toni at Mountain High Guiding Service as an independent contractor.

But before he'd hired her, they'd kissed twice. The first had been an awkward embrace in the ice cave at Fireweed Glacier back when she was in high school, and he was applying to online colleges. Beautiful but fleeting wild iris had filled the valley that day. He'd associated the purple blooms with her ever since.

Their second kiss had been at their friend Rabten's New Year's Eve party at Toklat Lodge. It'd happened last winter—after Toni had returned to Alaska but *before* they started working together. Did a New Year's kiss at midnight count? It did to him. He'd been replaying that night ever since. Toni probably hadn't thought twice about it. To others, it'd merely been a fun evening with friends, and a playful holiday tradition to ring in the new year.

He pushed those thoughts aside and agreed to the early staff meeting. A few moments later, his office door buzzed when Toni entered the code to the keyless lock they'd recently installed. The last thing he needed was unknowing staff or the public stumbling into his office while searching for the restrooms. The yeti community worked hard to stay undiscovered. If exposed, they risked the threat of monster hunters looking for trophies or white-suited government lab workers eager to experiment. As regional manager at Mountain High, Denzin took precautions.

Toni's sweet, floral scent perfumed the air as she entered. Denzin's heart thudded in time to the click of her knee-high boots across his office floor. Her long legs looked longer yet in tights and a sweater dress that hugged her tall, curvy figure. He snatched up his stress ball, a welcome distraction whenever Toni entered his office, and quickly tore his gaze away.

Eddie, a tall, blond, Viking-type who managed the Palmer office, followed Toni inside. "Your tux," he said, handing Denzin a garment bag. "Seems like a lot of formality for a small Alaska wedding. I'd be out of place in my fleece and Carhartts."

Toni's dark eyes twinkled, but Denzin didn't miss the abrupt frown as her phone buzzed. She glanced at the screen then quickly clicked it off. "My mom's coming up from Seattle for the wedding. I'd never hear the end of it if I went in anything but a dress, but you know someone will wear jeans and bunny boots. It's November in Alaska."

Denzin hung the garment bag next to his winter jacket as he agreed. "The Thanksgiving weekend forecast calls for subzero temperatures here in Wildwood, and even colder in the Interior. Julia and Wesley extended invitations around the state. People will bundle up, at least for their travel." Denzin often felt like an outsider around his brother and Julia, but he couldn't fault them for their inclusive celebration of yeti and yeti-friendly people.

Toni perched in a chair and arched an eyebrow. "Is the Alaska wedding for real, or just a party?"

"It's real and I'm officiating. I've obtained a marriage commissioner appointment for the celebration. They have a large reception planned later in California." Julia and Wes no longer lived in Alaska but had chosen to wed in the community where they first met and fell in love.

Eddie sat and laced his fingers behind his head before turning to Denzin. "Let me get this straight. Your mom was a yeti?"

"Correct."

"But your father was human, and after he and your mom separated, he had a second son, Wes, with a human, making you and Wes half-brothers?"

Denzin nodded. "That's right. Wes is about a year younger than me. I didn't meet him or my father until he and my mother reconciled and they moved in with us—me, my mom, and my maternal yeti grandparents—when I was in my teens."

Denzin and Wes weren't close, but there wasn't any bad blood between them, and neither had any other living family at this point. Having a human father and half-brother suddenly show up had taken some getting used to. Then Wes had left for college, and their father had moved back to California, unexpectedly dying shortly after. Wes had returned to Alaska for a few years as an adult, working at Mountain High. That was where he'd met Julia, an active outdoor enthusiast who, up until that point, had been casually dating Denzin.

Years had passed, and Denzin held no grudge

against his brother over Julia. He'd moved past old wounds and insecurities long ago—or so he'd thought.

Denzin understood why Julia chose Wes: Wes was human, and Denzin wasn't. Unlike his brother, Denzin couldn't attend a regular college or vie for "Alaska's Top Forty Under 40" with its required photos and public events. Honeymooning in the South of France, like Wes and Julia planned was impossible for Denzin. Sun, sand, and fur didn't mix, and Denzin didn't know any yeti who'd flown on a commercial jet.

While Denzin lowered his standing desk and tried to clear his thoughts, Eddie stretched out in his chair and said, "That's a wild family tree, Zin. Too bad I'll miss the party and the food. The weekend brunch at Fireweed is killer."

Denzin adjusted his slacks before he sat—it wouldn't do to stretch out the knees of his pants. Most yeti his age wore clothes, but few were as dressy as Denzin. He preferred business professional in the office even though he didn't meet with clients and would never partake in a video call. He might be a yeti, but no one who saw him could doubt his professionalism.

"I'll take your word for it," he said, crossing his legs as he opened a notebook. It wasn't like a yeti could saunter into a public restaurant on a random Sunday morning and do brunch. "Julia and Wes rented the entire Fireweed Glacier Chalet and Cabins for the weekend," Denzin explained. "A special catering crew is being brought in, and staff who don't know about yeti have been given those days off. We'll miss out on the famed mini quiche and dessert array."

Toni's phone vibrated, and she picked it up with an apology. "I forwarded the front desk phone to my cell. It might be the new guy, Jeremy. He's already had one warning for being late and then he didn't show this morning."

Denzin frowned both at the news and the sour look on Toni's face.

She set her phone down again and pasted what looked like a fake smile on her rosy lips. "Just my mom. She's, er, excited about the wedding." With two fingers rubbing at her temple, she went on. "We should discuss Jeremy, though. I'm trying to keep an open mind, but in addition to attendance issues, he's exhibited some problematic behaviors. He's struggling to learn the computer system, and needs instruction, but he doesn't like me directing him.

Also he dropped an f-bomb in front of a group of students yesterday."

Denzin growled in anger and frustration. Jeremy didn't know about yeti, so Toni was the next best person to train him—a job she was more than capable of. Denzin wouldn't tolerate abuse toward her or inappropriate behavior from his employees.

Toni further explained, "It was under his breath, at least. He quickly apologized and said it wouldn't happen again."

"It's disrespectful, nonetheless. And he's not here today, despite being on the schedule." Denzin steepled his fingers. He didn't like this, not one bit. "Jeremy is still in his probationary period. We could let him go."

With a shrug of a shoulder, Toni said, "We could. But I'd like to give him another chance. He may have a good reason for missing his shift."

Eddie snorted. "Not likely. I know the type. I *was* the type at that age. But it's your call, Denzin. Unfortunately, we can't spare any staff from the Palmer office."

Denzin reluctantly agreed to give Jeremy another chance, then shifted their focus to regular business. Today's agenda included holiday bonuses, sales numbers on guided trips into the Talkeetna and

Chugach Mountains, individual ski and ice climbing lessons, and local school visits. Kids loved the bouldering wall in the lobby that Toni had helped design. As their meeting wrapped up, all three of their phones sounded with incoming messages. They exchanged knowing grins.

"Bet a pitcher of beer it's Tseten," Eddie quipped as he dug his phone out of his pocket.

"No bet," Denzin and Toni both called out as they too reached for their phones. Tseten, their resident extroverted yeti, loved nothing better than getting a group of friends together.

> Tseten: Worked a deal with the brewery owner. Backroom secured. See you tonight.

The human Wildwood Brewery owner let them use her private event room for free when available. It had a separate entrance and staff were under strict instructions not to disturb guests. They ordered online, and a dumbwaiter delivered food and drink to the second-floor space. Perfect for yeti.

"Can't make it," Eddie lamented as he typed a response.

Toni had a murderous look on her face as she

tapped at her phone. "I need that beer now. My mother . . ." She let out a strangled sigh.

It pained Denzin to see her so agitated. "Anything I can do?" he asked, knowing he could do little besides buy her a drink tonight.

Toni offered a tight smile as she shook her head. "I just need a good session on the bouldering wall downstairs."

"Right? Go get it." Eddie fist bumped Toni as they all stood. "Has the city set a start date for construction on the climbing wall? I'm stoked to get on it. It's so rad that you won that grant."

Denzin might not have phrased it that way, but he agreed that Toni's achievements were impressive. Unlike him, she *would* make a great candidate for "Alaska's Top Forty Under 40." She'd secured approval from the city to build a full, multistory climbing wall at the Wildwood Recreation Center and had won a grant large enough to fund construction and several years of wages for employees. Denzin made a mental note to nominate her.

"Enjoy the Thanksgiving holiday weekend," Denzin said to Eddie. His fingers itched for the stress ball as his gaze connected with Toni's. "Have a good climbing session," he told her.

Once alone, Denzin ran a hand along his trim

whiskers trying to shake off his infatuation with Toni. But as he stared blankly at his computer, he pictured her downstairs in a sports bra and short shorts, skin shimmering with sweat and muscles flexing as she effortlessly—and gracefully—navigated the climbing holds.

He eyed the garment bag containing his tux. Gods, he needed a beer and an evening with friends. Plus, Toni would be there. He couldn't pursue anything with her, but he could at least enjoy her company tonight. He responded to Tseten's text with a thumbs up and typed a quick reply.

Denzin: I'll be there.

TONI YANKED on a pair of yellow rubber gloves, then snatched up a bottle of all-purpose cleaner and an abrasive sponge. She tackled the soap scum in her bathtub with all the fury of a daughter perfectly content with her life whose mother continuously insisted it was lacking.

"My house needs to shine before my mother arrives tomorrow," Toni ground out. Her arm muscles, already fatigued from her session on the bouldering wall, burned as she scoured the sides of the tub. "I don't want to give her anything else to criticize. And that new guy at work didn't show today— so aggravating." She scrubbed harder as she pictured Jeremy's sneering face.

Toni's friend Mari leaned against the bathroom doorframe. "Your cabin is already spotless."

Toni ignored the comment as she worked her way up a tiled wall with her sponge. "My mother nags me about being single and never acknowledges my accomplishments." Since moving back to Alaska a year ago, Toni had started her own business, signed a contract with Mountain High, and partnered with the city, winning a grant that would fund the area's first indoor climbing wall. None of these achievements had earned praise from her mother, not when Toni was still single.

"Your mother talks to mine, and believe me, she's proud of you. And Denzin's proud of you too— he let you build a bouldering wall at Mountain High. For the company, yeah, but also to help you demonstrate to the city what a climbing wall could be."

A warm glow spread through Toni at the reminder of Denzin's support. "Denzin has been great. But my mother never tells *me* she's proud.

Instead, I get constant reminders that I'm thirty, single, and my ovaries are drying up."

Mari took the stack of fresh towels off the counter and hung them on the rack. "I get that too—from the whole damn town it seems."

With a grimace, Toni paused her scrubbing. "Sorry, yeah. I guess you still get a lot of questions about Nima."

"So many. And he and I broke up years ago." Mari rolled her eyes and then asked, "Is your mother really pressuring you for grandkids?"

Toni released a harsh huff as she rinsed the bathtub. "Not in so many words, but do you know what she did today?"

Pausing while she emptied the garbage, Mari gave her the side-eye. "Do I want to know?"

Toni moved onto the sink, likely using twice as much cleaner as needed, her trigger finger hard to stop in her fury. "She joined a dating app with the sole purpose of finding single men for me. Apparently, she's found half a dozen matches within a fifty-mile radius of Wildwood and expects me to review her selections over the weekend while we're at the wedding." She plunged her hand into the soapy sink.

"Ah, shit."

"Right? Damn Wes and Julia for putting matrimonial ideas into my mother's head." Toni let out a sigh and reconsidered her finger pointing. "That's not fair of me. Mom was thrilled to receive an invitation." And she'd been looking forward to returning to the community where she'd raised Toni. "It isn't *their* fault."

"I dunno." Mari resumed her slouch against the doorframe. "I feel bad for Denzin. It can't be easy to see your ex marry your own brother. They didn't have to get married in Alaska."

Toni rinsed the sink. "They're making him wear a tux."

Mari grinned at that. "Of all the yeti we know, Denzin is one of the few who could pull off a tux with ease."

Toni's cheeks burned, and she quickly crouched to stash the cleaning supplies in the cabinet below the sink. Avoiding eye contact was key here. She couldn't reveal that she'd been daydreaming of Denzin, his snowy white fur stark against an ebony tux, since the staff meeting earlier. "I suppose," she squeaked.

The sight of him in formalwear would undoubtedly make her drool. With a trim beard that was more of a white five o'clock shadow against chiseled blue cheeks, and his broad shoulders and rock-hard body, there was no doubt she'd be stealing glances from afar at the wedding.

The truth was, her mother's unwavering insistence on finding her a romantic partner irked Toni because she was only interested in one person, er, yeti—Denzin. He'd been her first kiss when she was a gangly teenager complete with braces. Their relationship hadn't progressed beyond that, though—she'd been too busy with her first part-time job, and he'd spent the rest of the summer out of town with other yeti.

More recently, before she'd gone to work for him, they'd shared a kiss to ring in the new year. It hardly counted since most of the partygoers had embraced their closest neighbor at midnight. But her and Denzin's kiss hadn't been on the cheek. It had been a slow and deliberate brush of lips. There'd been heat, a sizzle below the surface, and a smolder in Denzin's steel-blue eyes that she'd recalled repeatedly over the passing months—especially late at night in bed when her hand traveled southward.

Damn, I need to stop thinking of him that way! It didn't matter that they'd both been single since she'd returned to Alaska. She'd worked hard to start her own business and earn respect from the community. She didn't need a workplace relationship to jeopardize her reputation. What if the city leaders began to doubt her or question her choices?

No, nothing could ever happen with Denzin now, given their new working relationship. Besides, maybe she'd imagined the heat between them last New Year's Eve. He'd certainly never said anything about it.

Mari's phone chimed, pulling Toni from her thoughts. She stopped pretending to rearrange cleaning products in the cabinet and stood, watching her friend frown as she typed a message into her phone. "Something wrong?" Toni asked.

"No, it's just that I recently made a new friend, Gina. But she doesn't know about yeti, so . . ."

Toni grimaced in return. "So Gina's not invited to the brewery tonight."

"Sadly, no. But I should introduce you. She needs friends. We'll have a girl's night sometime." Mari looked up. "But right now, we need beer and good company. And to not think about annoying coworkers, nagging mothers, or biological clocks."

Toni groaned. "I'm so on board with that."

Mari gave Toni's legs a pointed look. "You going to the brewery in your sweats?"

Right. She'd put on yoga pants to clean the bathroom. Toni guided Mari into her small living room, then ran upstairs to change clothes. Denzin would be at the brewery, which meant Toni needed to carefully choose her outfit. The yeti of her dreams was off-limits, but that didn't mean she couldn't look her best tonight.

CHAPTER TWO

W hen Denzin entered the private room at Wildwood Brewery, Tseten greeted him with a wide smile and a pitcher of beer. Denzin ordered a second, Polar Pilsner, Toni's favorite.

With a frosty mug in hand, Denzin clinked his glass to Tseten's. "Thanks for arranging this tonight," he said, tension easing after the first cold sip.

"It's what I do. My happy place." Tseten loved people, and gods knew the yeti community benefited from his outgoing nature. But a yeti could only know so many people—Tseten's strength would always be limited.

Denzin hung his jacket on the back of a chair and took a seat. "How's Rosa?" Tseten owned a successful computer programming business. His human girlfriend lived in California and didn't know that her long-distance romantic partner *and* remote work colleague happened to be covered head to toe in white fur. Aside from the small headshot that appeared when Rosa sent Tseten an email, they hadn't shared images of each other. Tseten couldn't, not that Rosa knew that. But for now, they both seemed content with their arrangement.

Tseten grinned, his eyes not meeting Denzin's, as if Rosa's name had triggered a private thought. "She's great. This year she's in charge of the Thanksgiving dessert for her family's dinner. We both tested a sweet potato pie recipe last weekend. It passed. She'll make that and a cranberry tiramisu. I sent both recipes to Pema."

Denzin chuckled. Tseten's cousin was an excellent cook and ran her own catering company. "I hope Pema shares. Was she put out that Wes and Julia didn't ask Blue Lotus to cater the wedding?"

Tseten sipped at his mug and shook his head. "Nah, she understands they wanted her to be a guest instead." He paused. "Are Wes and Julia in town yet?"

Denzin focused on his beer. "They arrive tomorrow."

"And you're okay with everything?"

Denzin stifled a sigh. Not another of Tseten's "feelings" talks. Of course Denzin wasn't okay, but he wasn't going to admit it to Tseten. "Why wouldn't I be?"

The outside door squeaked open and a gust of cold air swept across the room interrupting them.

But that didn't stop Tseten. "You're marrying your ex to your human half-brother—the guy who has all the advantages in life that a yeti will never have."

"Ouch, Tset." Mari broke the silence as she and Toni walked up. Great. Like he needed a reminder of his undesirability—especially in front of Toni. How had his life come to this?

Tseten raised his hands in surrender as the women joined them at the table and helped themselves to beer. "It's not Denzin's fault. I'm just saying that this weekend has to suck for him, that's all."

"It's gonna suck for all of us. Isn't that why we're drinking tonight?" Mari asked. She worried the chain around her neck. "I've been happily single for years. Yet people at the wedding will *still* ask me about Nima. They associate me with him."

She had a point. The community still thought of them as a couple, despite their separation.

Mari gestured to Toni, who'd taken the seat

across from Denzin, next to Tseten. "At least I won't have to deal with my mother trying to set me up with random men all weekend."

Toni's face turned the color of a deep crimson sunset as she clamped a hand to her forehead. "My mom joined a dating app to find guys for me."

Denzin's shoulders stiffened. Toni date? The thought of her mother pushing eligible human men toward her made his blood run cold.

Tseten slid a friendly arm around her shoulders, and she sagged into him. Envy pricked at Denzin. He wanted to comfort Toni—and keep all suitors at bay.

"It was thoughtful of Wes and Julia to invite her, but now she wants to spend their wedding weekend planning *my* eventual nuptials."

Denzin didn't like the idea of Toni dating, period, but it wasn't like he could date her. They worked together, and he was a yeti. His ex had made it clear that he had nothing to offer a human woman. *I need to get over Toni already.*

"And let's not forget about you, Tseten," Mari added. "You're attending the wedding with a friend, me, and your cousin, Pema, because your partner hasn't seen you—ever. She doesn't even know what you are."

Tseten scowled before slugging back his beer.

Mari looked around the table. "What a sad lot we are."

Ugh. Mari wasn't wrong.

"At least you'll have each other," Toni observed as she motioned between Tseten and Mari. "Denzin and I are dateless. And no. My mother doesn't count as a date."

They sat in silence for a moment, presumably all stewing in their own self-pity, when Tseten sat up straight. "You don't have to be," he said.

Toni's brow furrowed. "Don't have to be what?"

"Dateless. Alone. You and Denzin can go together as friends. Just like me, Mari, and Pema. Or if you want your mom off your back, tell her you're dating, but you've kept it a secret because you weren't ready to go public."

Toni's eyes grew wide. "I work for Denzin. He holds my contract. That's like dating the boss."

Tseten cocked his head. "Is it, though? I'm aware of the gray area surrounding office relationships. But we're all friends first, right? Besides, it would also help Denzin. Let him show Julia that he's moved on and up. It seems like you'd each have something to gain by attending together as a couple. Even if it's fake."

Denzin glanced at Toni, her dark glossy hair tumbling over her shoulders, the plunging V-neck of her shirt that he should *not* be staring at, and those plump, kissable lips. Beneath all that was a brilliant mind and a warm heart. She was so much better than Julia. But Denzin didn't play games, and he certainly didn't want to make Toni uncomfortable. "That's unnecessary," he assured her.

"This weekend could be better with someone at your side," Tseten argued. "You two could easily fake a believable relationship. You've known each other forever."

It was usually Denzin's job to make persuasive arguments. Hell, he'd recently convinced a large tour company to book their summer land-based glacier excursions with Mountain High. A huge win for the company and Wildwood. But tonight, it seemed the roles had been reversed.

They had to be realistic. Life would go on after this weekend. "Lying about a relationship won't help anyone in the long run."

"It *is* a wild suggestion," Mari added, "but I'm seeing the benefits for you both."

Toni, who seemed to avoid Denzin's gaze, took a large sip of her beer before giving Mari a hard look. "You think it's fine for me to fake date Denzin?"

Mari scowled. "Like Tseten said, we all grew up together. We're friends. And we'll be there to help you with it. It's only for the weekend. Both of you will have a better time together. Then, when everyone leaves, it's over."

Toni gave a harsh laugh. "And the coach turns back into a pumpkin," she said, just before her phone lit up. They all saw the text from her mother and the images of the dating candidates. Toni hesitated before clicking on one. A picture of a shirtless man in a ball cap holding a freshly caught salmon filled the screen.

Oh, hell no.

Mari covered her mouth with her hand. "There is so much wrong with that picture." She turned to Denzin. "Save her, Zin."

Denzin regarded Toni. Of course he'd love to spend the weekend with her as his date, real or otherwise. But was that the right thing to do? Did Toni want it? He glanced at the picture on her phone again, and it suddenly didn't matter to him what was right or wrong. He wanted Toni for himself—if she'd have him. "Okay," he said. "I'm in."

TONI STARED AT DENZIN, his steel-blue gaze locked with hers. Had he just agreed to be her fake boyfriend for his brother's wedding? She resisted the urge to squirm in her chair as her body heated.

Tearing her eyes away, she glanced down at the picture on her phone and suppressed a shudder. She wanted nothing to do with the guys her mother had chosen. *I want Denzin.* But he was her boss, technically. Off limits. Should they even pretend?

While Denzin gave her space to think, Mari didn't. "Girl, what say you?" she begged. With a waggle of her eyebrows, she added, "Having a date for the weekend, real or not, sounds like a good time to me."

Be at Denzin's side for several days? Toni's heart leaped, telling her to do it, try it, take advantage, and get to know Zin even better. Meanwhile, the worrier inside tried to slam the brakes. Fake relationships were for the movies. And pretending to date at the wedding could make things weird afterward—especially with people who didn't know the truth. She didn't want to jeopardize her professional reputation.

She rubbed at her face with both hands. She'd been living safe for so long. Too long. The likelihood of any significant consequences was remote. Maybe she should take a chance. Do something daring. It *would* be a good time—if they pulled it off.

Toni dropped her hands and looked at Denzin, his focus still on her. "Okay. Let's do it."

Full, sky-blue lips curled into a smile aimed right at her. She'd been flushed before, now her internal temperature shot to approximately one thousand.

Mari clapped, then raised her glass. "Cheers to the fake couple."

"To friends," Tseten added.

Denzin raised his glass. "To success."

Toni let out a breath and joined in. "To no drama."

They all drank, then Denzin grabbed his phone. "Can I have your mother's number, Toni? With your permission, I'm going to start our charade now and respectfully request that she stop sending pictures of men to my girlfriend."

Girlfriend? I like that label way too much. Toni couldn't have stopped the grin if she'd wanted to. "You have my permission. But copy me on the text. I want to see my mom's reaction."

He gave a nod. "Of course."

Tseten chuckled. "I wish there were blind copies on texts. I also want to see how Bev reacts—if she doesn't respond immediately."

Denzin picked up his phone and typed a message. He showed it to Toni for her approval and Tseten leaned over her shoulder to read it as well.

> Denzin: Hello Bev, Denzin here. Toni and I were waiting to share our news until everyone arrived . . . We are dating. I'm not the jealous type, however, I don't want to see any more eligible bachelor pics popping up on my girlfriend's phone. She's off the market. Safe travels, we'll see you tomorrow.

Toni fought a pleased smile, then nodded at Denzin, indicating he should hit send. "Shall we bet to see how long it takes—" She didn't finish her sentence before her mother responded. Denzin read the text aloud to everyone.

> Bev: Very funny, Toni. I think the guy with the fish . . . they all have fish. The guy on the big boat with the fish is *100*.

That wiped the smile off her face.

"What the hell?" Denzin scowled at his phone. "She doesn't believe us."

Mari wagged a finger at the two of them. "You need to send a selfie."

Denzin gave a curt nod of agreement and crooked a finger at Toni. "C'mere."

Denzin beckoning to her. She would replay that move later tonight and many more nights to come. She rounded the table and leaned in next to him, careful to keep some distance, but he pulled her closer, the feel of his arms wrapped around her setting her skin on fire.

"I think you should sit on my lap. We need to sell this."

Toni swallowed her response—they were lying after all—and eyed Denzin's massive dark rinse, jean-clad thighs. Where did he shop? Were they custom made like his tuxedo? If she sat on his lap, the heat of him would soak into her body. His sandalwood and juniper scent would wrap around her, and she might swoon on the spot.

When she was slow to move, he glanced over at her. "Would you rather not? I apologize if I made you uncomfortable."

Oh god. Awkward. Tseten and Mari watched with stupidly amused grins. Toni slid onto Denzin's lap. The heat from his hard, muscular thighs *did* soak into her like a sweet infusion while his nearness made her pulse jump. "No, no. It's fine." She tried her best to flash a bright smile his way, but his face was so close she could hardly focus on it, and her smile likely looked more like constipation. "This is a good plan."

Mari rolled her eyes. "You two. Set your phone down, Zin. I'll take some pictures and send them to you." She called out various poses—Toni's hand on Denzin's chest, his arms wrapped around her, their cheeks flush against each other.

His short stiff fur created a delicious friction against her skin when he moved his head. Toni would never forget the sensation.

Then Denzin surprised her by placing a slow, full-lipped kiss near the corner of her mouth, and she nearly melted into him. Her nerve endings came alive and she closed her eyes, reveling in the moment's bliss.

"Aw yeah. That's the money shot," Mari declared.

Tseten whistled. "That should stop Bev in her tracks."

When Denzin slowly drew away, warmth lingered on Toni's cheek from his lips. She blinked rapidly, trying to ground herself. *This is fake, Toni. Don't forget it!*

Still, she wanted to ask Mari for a copy of *all* the pictures. Something to scroll through when she was alone and could daydream to her heart's content. She saw one picture—the shot Denzin quickly forwarded to Toni and her mother.

> Denzin: I'm serious Bev. No more. She's mine.

If only. Toni watched three dots appear on Denzin's screen. Her mother was responding. The dots disappeared and came back.

> Bev: You two are serious?

Under his breath, Denzin said, "I just said we were. I wouldn't be anything but serious about your daughter."

Awareness prickled as Toni processed his words. But they were pretending. Denzin meant nothing by it. He only wanted her mom to think he was sincere.

> Denzin: Completely. See you tomorrow.

Toni slid off Denzin's warm lap, immediately missing his heat, scent, the closeness of his body. "We're committed now. Next up, your family."

She let out a slow breath. This was happening. Toni and Denzin were now a fake couple.

CHAPTER THREE

Denzin pulled his truck into Toni's driveway. The sun hadn't yet risen, but a golden glow on the horizon signaled the approaching midmorning dawn. He clenched the steering wheel. What the fuck was he doing? What were they doing?

Last night, they'd told Toni's mother they were dating. And while lying about a relationship didn't sit well with Denzin, he was glad they'd done it, if only to put an end to her mother's matchmaking. It also gave him the chance to treat Toni like a girlfriend. At least for a few days.

His phone buzzed. He plucked it from his pocket as he climbed out of his truck, snow crunching under his winter boots. It buzzed again before he navigated to a group text with Toni, Mari, and Tseten.

> Tseten: Bev is doing her homework. Zin & Toni, she texted me to check your story.

> Mari: She called my mom. I told her that D+T= *red heart*

Denzin looked up from the message. Toni stood in her front window, phone in hand, watching him. A slow smile brightened her face, and she motioned for him to come inside.

He'd only been to Toni's a handful of times. A hill and a stand of aspen trees surrounding the two-story cabin provided enough privacy that the neighbors couldn't see Denzin. Otherwise, he would have lifted his hood to hide his furry head and blue face.

Toni opened the door, and they exchanged greetings as she ushered him inside. As soon as the door shut, a silent, awkward beat passed. A pink hue stained Toni's cheeks as she stole a glance up at him. Denzin might be head to toe muscle, but that little look made his insides flutter. It was one thing to be alone in the office with her, it was another to be in her home without their buffer of friends.

He cleared his throat. "Are you okay with this arrangement?" he asked at the same time she asked, "Still want to go through with this?"

"Yes," they both said simultaneously.

They laughed like nervous teenagers. *Gods.* But Toni's giggle faded into a smile so sweet it made his teeth ache.

"Since that's settled," she said, "want a cup of coffee before we go to the chalet? It will give us time to come up with a story. You know, decide how long we've been seeing each other and all that."

Her place was warm, cozy, and smelled of cinnamon and freshly brewed coffee. He eyed her worn couch, imagining himself stretched out on it with her in his arms. He gave his head a mental shake. *No matter how much I want her for real, this is pretend.* He had to maintain that boundary, even if for his own sanity.

But there was nothing wrong with having an innocent cup of coffee with a friend—so they could concoct a lie. He suppressed a groan. "I'd love some. And good idea. People will ask for details."

"It's only natural for them to be curious." She led him to the kitchen, then filled two mugs. Denzin sat across from her at a small table, and she passed him a cloth-covered basket, drawing back the edges to reveal thick slices of spiced bread.

He inhaled deeply before helping himself to one. "This smells delicious. Did you make it?"

Toni took a piece for herself. "I wish, but no. Mari gave me leftovers from the retirement center kitchen."

Denzin frowned. "She's never given *me* leftovers."

Toni let out a soft laugh, likely because of his envious tone. "Mostly she takes them to Dorje these days."

He lowered his bread to his plate. "How is Dorje? I've reached out, but he hasn't spoken to me since the accident. I'm holding his job, of course. He did nothing wrong. He was the hero."

"We all know that. Hopefully Dorje will figure it out with time. Tseten visits him. As far as I can tell, Tseten talks, and Dorje doesn't." She paused and smiled. "Last night, Tseten was wearing the Viking hat that Dorje knit for him."

The corner of Denzin's mouth lifted. "The most mileage any Halloween costume has ever gotten." And likely a show of support for a fellow yeti and their friend, Dorje, who'd had a challenging year. Not only had he lost the human grandmother who'd raised him, but he'd also been involved in a mountaineering accident—a stark reminder of life's fleeting nature. All the more reason not to fret over a pretend relationship. If it made an uncomfortable weekend easier, and hopefully fun, why not do it?

Toni sipped from her mug. "So . . . how long have we been dating? Since this fall?"

"Should it be longer?"

"Maybe. Remember that hike we all did this summer at the pass outside Palmer?" Toni paused, her mug halfway to her mouth. "Wait. That was a work thing, wasn't it? We can't consider that a date."

Denzin scratched his head. "Right, yeah. We could say something vague, like, it's been coming on slowly."

She rewarded him with a smile. "I like that. It's probably best to not give many details anyway. We don't want to inadvertently forget our story or contradict each other."

Denzin chuckled as he finished his bread. "We spend so much time together that our stories should align if we're pressed for details. Faking a relationship will be a breeze, and the weekend will be over before we know it." Perhaps too quickly, but he'd take what he could get.

Toni nodded. "Tonight is cocktails and appetizers before the rehearsal dinner. Tomorrow is Thanksgiving and the wedding day, complete with the reception dinner and party. Brunch follows on

Friday. And my mom is here for the entire weekend. If we part ways after Friday, she might question the authenticity of our relationship."

"I'm helping with wedding prep this afternoon but I'm free on Saturday and Sunday. You're off the hook with my family over the weekend. Wes and Julia leave for their honeymoon on Friday night."

Toni gave a nod and let out a breath. "Well," she said. "I can't thank you enough for helping me out. Moving to Alaska, over a thousand miles from my mother, wasn't enough distance to stop her from intruding in my life. I'm sorry if Tseten and Mari strong-armed you into this."

He held up a hand. "They didn't. And no apology is necessary. I'm glad I can help. Remember that you're doing something for me as well, you know. I'm not uh . . ." He ran a hand across the back of his neck, his collar suddenly irritating his fur. "I didn't want to be the ex, the brother of the groom, and the only single guy in the room. It's difficult for me to admit, but it's true."

Toni crossed her arms and rested them on the table. "We're in this together then. I'm telling myself to have fun with it and stop worrying."

A frown tugged at Denzin's mouth. "What are you worried about? Our work situation or that someone will doubt our story? If you're not comfortable with this, we don't have to go through with it. We can tell your mother we broke up and that you're not ready to date again."

With a grimace she said, "I have a bad habit of worrying about everything. I'm overreacting. It's nothing." Another rosy streak colored her cheeks. "I want to do this," she insisted, pushing back from the table. "We should probably get going."

Denzin nodded in agreement. Hopefully she wasn't suffering any serious misgivings.

They washed their dishes, and Denzin carried Toni's bags to his truck, hanging her garment bag next to his in the backseat. While driving to the event, they tried to recall all the things they'd done together over summer and fall—potential dates. But most of it blurred the lines between work and activities with friends, some of whom they also worked with.

When they pulled up to the chalet to unload their bags, a small crowd emerged from the entrance, including Bev, Wes, and Julia. Apparently, he and Toni were more interesting than the bride and groom.

"Antoinette," Bev cried as she inched down the snowy stairs toward the truck. She swatted Denzin on the arm as she passed him. "Dating in secret? My daughter is too good to hide."

Toni flashed Denzin a wide-eyed, apologetic look as she hugged her mother. "Mom, enough. Denzin and I both agreed to keep our relationship private. Our feelings on the matter were mutual."

Bev grumbled, but requested a begrudging hug from Denzin. "It's good to see you and your brother. I will never forget how quickly you two could empty my fridge."

He offered her a wide smile. "Thank you for keeping it full."

Wes stepped forward to shake Denzin's hand. Julia, with a flip of her long blond hair, followed, offering Denzin a gentle hug and air kisses on both cheeks. He'd seen the couple many times over the years they'd been dating. Most of the initial awkwardness had faded, but he was damn glad he wasn't standing there alone. He didn't want their pity for his furry, still single, and lonely state.

Julia clasped her hands together. "We were thrilled to hear your news. We shared the airport shuttle to the chalet with Bev, and she filled us in. Introduce me to your girlfriend."

Denzin pasted what he hoped was a casual smile on his face. "Certainly. Julia, this is Antoinette."

Toni shook Julia's hand. "Please call me Toni. And congratulations, you've chosen a beautiful setting for an Alaska wedding."

Denzin moved on to his brother. "Toni, you remember Wes?"

"Of course." Toni gave him a quick hug. "It's been years. Great to see you again, Wes, and under such happy circumstances. But you all must be freezing. We should take our bags inside."

Julia laid a hand on Toni's shoulder and pointed toward a collection of snowy structures that lined the drive. "You and Denzin will be in an outbuilding. The guests scheduled for the Aurora cabin couldn't make it. Now it's yours." She winked at her. "It's the most secluded."

Blood drained from Denzin's face as he eyed the distant cabin.

Crap. They hadn't talked about sleeping arrangements. He'd assumed that Toni would still room with her mother.

After an awkward hesitation, he turned to Toni, her strained smile likely identical to his. They scooted toward each other in the snow, hands colliding as they both tried to wrap an arm around the other.

"How very, er, thoughtful of you, Julia," Toni replied.

Denzin quickly nodded and gave a completely honest response. "Yes, what a, um . . . surprise."

INSIDE THEIR QUAINT CABIN, Toni stood next to Denzin, bags in hand, her gaze fixated on the enormous bed in the room's corner. The *one* enormous bed.

Toni tingled with awareness. Was this a good development or a bad one? Her heart and hormones had popped the champagne—*good*, they screamed. The worrier in her needed an antacid. "My mom and I were supposed to share a double-bed chalet room. It didn't occur to me they'd change things around."

Denzin blew out a breath. "I had a single room in the chalet with a twin."

Toni's free hand slid to her hip, annoyance drowning out her warring emotions. "You can't comfortably fit in a twin bed. That was shitty of Wes and Julia. You're family, *and* you're marrying them."

Denzin shrugged and took Toni's garment bag from her, hanging it in the closet. "I'm sure space is limited. And don't worry, I'll be fine on the floor. I'm a yeti, after all. I've got fur to keep me warm."

Toni rounded on him, mouth agape. She would *never* make him sleep on the floor. "No, absolutely not. It's a big bed. We shared a bed in the camper when we drove to Denali for the Halloween party a few weeks ago. This is no big deal."

That wasn't true, at least not for Toni. Five of them had slept in the camper, all in their own sleeping bags and within view of one another. On the mattress she and Denzin shared, his head had been at her feet and vice versa.

This was a proper bed with sheets, a fluffy duvet, and lots of pillows. Sharing this bed *would* be a big deal to her. And truth be told, Toni wanted to slide under the sheets with Denzin and wake up in his arms—or at least with their heads sharing the same end of the bed. Her inner worrier could stuff it.

Denzin ducked his head and looked away. "You're very considerate. Should we unpack?"

Together, they emptied their bags. There was an unexpected intimacy in arranging their personal belongings in the room they'd share for the next few days and Toni fought a feeling of shyness.

The cabin had two plush chairs next to a narrow table, an electric kettle and a basket with tea, hot chocolate, and instant coffee packets. The window next to the door overlooked the snowy path to the chalet. In the corner, the rustic, wooden bedframe dominated the room.

A large half mirror spanned the length of the bed. A shame it didn't reach the floor. Toni would have liked to see her full-length reflection before the wedding. She paused. That probably wasn't the purpose of the mirror anyway in this *secluded* cabin.

"I wonder why this is called the Aurora cabin?" she mused as she opened the drawers under the electric kettle. One held an old Wildwood summer guide and a brochure for Mountain High Guiding Service. She grinned at the photo of Eddie on the cover before dropping it back in the drawer and opening the next.

"The artwork?" Denzin guessed, gesturing to a picture of the northern lights partially hidden behind the bathroom door.

Toni moved to the nightstand and noted an even smaller photo of the night sky. "I think you're right," she agreed as she slid the top drawer open. "Here's another."

Denzin came up behind her, presumably to see the photo, but they both peered into the open drawer where a long sleeve of condoms lay curled on itself.

"Someone had fun in here," she remarked, attempting to add a hint of levity to their find and steer her thoughts away from sex with Denzin. *And now I'm blushing.* "Or they *didn't*," she added with a forced laugh, "since they left all their condoms."

Denzin picked them up. "The expiration date is years from now. These are new. And—" He looked at her and seemed to change what he was going to say. "If you take any, just, er . . . make sure they're sized correctly for your partner." He stepped away and pulled on his jacket. "I'm going to check in with Wes and Julia to see what they need done. I'll be back in time for appetizers."

The door quickly opened and closed, and Toni stood there, staring at the condom packets in her hand and the labeling that read "XXL." Even with no witnesses to see her embarrassment, the heat of a blush swept up her neck. Extra, extra-large for a giant yeti dick. That's what Denzin hadn't said. They were meant to sheath someone his size, not some average human erection.

Ho-boy. What have I gotten myself into?

CHAPTER FOUR

After helping organize the flower arrangements, Toni slipped back to her and Denzin's cabin for a shower and to get ready for the evening.

She'd briefly spotted Denzin earlier when he was helping unload flowers, but Julia had since sent him off on another errand, and he hadn't returned to the room yet. Her gaze snagged on the bed, then drifted to the drawer full of condoms as she made her way into the bathroom.

What did it mean that she tingled at the idea of her and Denzin using those condoms? Simple. She found Denzin attractive, and a girl got horny from time to time. Basic science. A drawer full of condoms didn't mean they *had* to have sex. Having ice cream in the freezer didn't mean one had to eat a bowl full either. But who'd deny themselves ice cream?

Ugh. Not helpful. Now she wanted sex with Denzin *and* ice cream. Preferably both, together.

Toni undressed for her shower, but as she pulled the curtain back to step into the tub, the rod and curtain came crashing down. The rusty shower hooks no longer closed completely, leaving the curtain detached in places, and the stubborn rod refused to stay in the holder. As she was wrangling it back into place, a knock sounded at the front door, then Denzin's voice filled the cabin.

"It's me. I'm back."

A smile tugged at Toni's lips. Denzin was "home" while she stood naked in the shower. Well, nearly in the shower. "I'm about to wash up," she called. "Just fixing the shower curtain rod."

His deep voice sounded from the other side of the bathroom door. "Need a hand?"

Toni glanced down at her stiffening nipples and nearly groaned at her lack of control. They'd hardened at the sound of his voice and his nearness. "Um. Nope. Got it. Thanks."

After a few more adjustments, the rod held, and Toni stepped into the shower. As she moved under the hot stream, her thoughts returned to Denzin.

Had she ever stopped thinking about him? What was he doing in the other room? Was he also thinking about the drawer *full* of condoms? Probably not. The man was the definition of respect and discipline.

Toni had just begun to rinse the shampoo out of her hair when the rod fell again—this time on her, the rusty, open hooks catching in her hair on its way down. She yelped, snatching the rod before it ripped out a chunk of her hair.

A moment later, Denzin burst through the bathroom door. "Are you okay?"

She couldn't see him from her position—bent at the waist, hair in her eyes and water pelting her back —as she held the rod next to her head, trying desperately with her free hand to untangle her hair from the hooks that pinched and pulled. "Ouch! One of the hooks is caught in my hair."

Denzin sucked in a breath before the weight of the rod eased from her hands, and the shower stopped. "Let me see," he rumbled right next to her very naked, very exposed body.

Oh, god. Nipples, do not react to him. Do not! A slight tug on her hair brought her focus back. She'd have a hard time untangling herself. She needed his help. "Thank you. This damn rod. It won't stay up." She rubbed her abused scalp. "That actually hurt."

Denzin emitted a low growl. "Your hair is wound around two hooks. The hotel needs to fix this rod and replace the old hardware."

Large, blue feet and white-furred legs stepped into the tub next to her. Right, so they were now in the shower together—her naked and Denzin . . . Well, his legs were bare. She tried to raise her head a fraction, her eyes tracking up his legs to see just how bare they were. Her gaze stopped at a band of gray— the hem of his boxer briefs. Her mouth twitched in satisfaction. So that's what he wore beneath his work slacks.

"Easy, I've almost got it," he said, pulling her thoughts back to the situation.

Gentle fingers worked through her hair, and quickly freed her. As Denzin busied himself with the rod, Toni straightened, getting an eyeful of Denzin. Evidently, he'd caught some shower spray. His boxer briefs clung to what looked like a solid gluteus maximus that she wanted to run her hands over.

She didn't touch him, of course. Instead, she used her hands to cover herself, though he didn't give her a glance, his focus on the troublesome rod.

"This isn't going to stay up long," he grumbled, then turned to her, his gaze never straying below her face. "Let me see your head. Did the rod break the skin when it hit you?"

Toni shuffled forward, her feet moving on their own accord at Denzin's request. She leaned her head toward him. "Right here," she said, her fingers gliding over a sore spot above her left ear.

A low growl vibrated from Denzin's chest—his wet, toned chest—that Toni had braced herself against. Really, she had no choice, nowhere else for her hands to go, as he gently parted her hair, inspecting what felt like a small bump.

While his fingers danced over her head, Toni tentatively moved her hand a fraction—surely not a noticeable amount. Muscles flexed and soft fur glided beneath her palm. *And I'm a total creeper copping a feel . . . but he feels so good.*

"It doesn't seem to be bleeding," Denzin murmured, his lips mere inches from her ear.

He'd moved his hand, she realized. It now cradled the side of her face.

Toni couldn't help it. She closed her eyes and leaned into his caress, loving his touch.

"Toni," he whispered, his voice husky. She nearly moaned in response as her eyes fluttered open, water droplets framing her lashes. Denzin looked down at her through hooded, deep blue, bedroom eyes.

It wasn't her nipples grabbing her attention at that moment, but her heart. It clenched and spasmed at the thrill and fear of the situation they'd gotten themselves into and where it might lead.

Then the shower curtain rod fell again.

TONI CRIED out and jumped away from Denzin and the falling rod. She covered herself with her hands, shielding her body from his view. Those small, hot hands that had just been on *his* body. His skin burned where she'd pressed her palms against him, as if her simple touch had branded him.

Whatever spell they'd been under had shattered with the falling rod.

But Denzin hadn't missed the look in Toni's eyes, a mix of desire or apprehension. He'd also noticed how her teeth snagged her plump lip. A lip he'd nearly kissed. Again.

Determined to keep his gaze off Toni, he quickly stepped out of the tub and raised the curtain, blocking her from his view. "I'll hold this, you finish," he said. His words were gruffer than intended as he fought to regain control of his body and calm his racing heart.

Her shadow didn't move. "Are you sure?" she asked.

"Of course. You have shampoo in your hair and only just started your shower. I'll fix this when you're done." *And not standing next to me . . . naked.*

"I'll hurry," Toni insisted, and Denzin realized he could see her silhouette quite well as she tipped her head back into the stream of water, her fingers diving into those dark locks he'd been caressing a mere moment ago.

He slammed his eyes shut. "It's no problem," he ground out, adjusting his grip on the curtain rod. "Take all the time you need." Gods knew he needed a moment to get himself under control. His dick had dropped, and his wet boxers hid nothing, the fabric outlining an aching erection. Of course the rod had fallen as he was changing out of snow-dampened jeans and into sweatpants. It didn't help that before he'd jumped into the shower to help a naked Toni, he'd been thinking about the condoms next to their soon-to-be-shared bed. Thinking about the different ways he and Toni might use them.

Stop picturing Toni naked and open your eyes. But he could see naked shadow Toni reaching for a bottle by the side of the tub. Eyes open or closed, he was screwed.

He needed to get his mind off her body. "Did, uh, you finish with the flowers?" he asked, trying his hardest to sound normal, casual. As if he hadn't just seen Toni naked and wasn't hanging out with her while she showered.

Toni huffed a laugh. "Yes, but I'm not sure they met Julia's satisfaction." Her voice sounded more like her usual self, which helped even out Denzin's erratic breathing.

"Did you get everything done?" Toni asked. "I kind of got the impression that Julia . . . well, it's not fair of me to judge. I don't know her."

"I felt like the errand boy," he admitted with a sigh. Just thinking about Julia, Wes, and their wedding was a definite boner killer. Depressing, but welcome at the moment.

Toni's head poked out from behind the curtain, and she smirked. "I knew it. That bitch."

Denzin grinned. "Finish your shower."

She grinned in return, then ducked back under the water. "You'll love this." She paused, and a tube sputtered. "Julia asked if we'd been dating over my birthday and what you'd gotten me."

"She's a little superficial."

"Ya think?"

"You took your birthday off and went hiking with Mari. I ordered coffee and your favorite pastries for the office the day before."

Toni went quiet. Too quiet. "You knew it was my birthday?"

"June twenty-first. Summer solstice. Yeah, I knew. I should have said something," he admitted, feeling a little sheepish now.

She stuck her head out again. "Thank you. Your gesture made my day—twice. Both then and now." She hesitated, then closed the curtain once more. "I figured Julia only cared how much you spent. I told her you sent me a gigantic bouquet of tropical flowers and cooked dinner for me. She said you'd never cooked for her." Toni gave a delighted laugh as she turned the water off. "I know this isn't a competition, but I won that round."

Denzin couldn't help the gratified grin that pulled at his lips. It felt good to have someone in his corner for a change. "I'll admit, I find satisfaction in that on many levels. Sounds like I owe you flowers and dinner then."

Toni chuckled. "How about a towel, and we call it even?"

With one hand, Denzin pulled a towel from the

rack and passed it to Toni behind the curtain. Then he grabbed the other towel, letting it drape from his arm to cover . . . Well, he'd only cooled off so much.

Toni stepped out of the tub wrapped from chest to thigh, her skin glowing.

Denzin lowered the rod and curtain, resting them in the tub, as an urge to explain Julia to Toni niggled at him. "I want you to know," he said, adjusting his towel to better conceal his, uh, excited parts. "Julia and I were never in love."

Toni locked eyes with him. "You don't have to explain. She wasn't a good fit, but it still hurts to be—"

"Dumped."

Her gaze didn't waver. "You're better off—better, period. She isn't your type."

"You know my type?" His voice came out huskier than he'd intended. He knew his type, without a doubt. She stood in front of him, naked save for the thin towel draped around her delicious body. It thrilled him to think that Toni had paid close enough attention to have insight on the matter.

Her throat worked as she swallowed, a simple movement that affected him enough that he had to tighten his grip on his towel. "I know it well," she whispered.

She paused a beat, then gestured to the rod. "You need me to—"

"Nah, I'll get it up," he said, inwardly rolling his eyes when he realized the innuendo. He had no trouble getting it up around Toni.

Seemingly unaware of where his thoughts had gone, she gave a quick nod. Then Toni stepped past him and closed the door behind her, leaving him to fix the curtain and take his own shower—which, now, needed to be ice cold.

TONI CINCHED her towel around her body and plopped down on the bed. It'd been twenty hours since she and Denzin had agreed to this arrangement, which hadn't left them much time to figure out all the details. Still, she'd pictured sitting next to him at the reception dinner, dancing, and generally acting like a couple in front of her mother.

Not once had she imagined palming his bare chest while she stood next to him buck-ass naked.

Toni had a decision to make. It was one thing to act like a romantic couple in front of others. It was another to get flirty in the shower. Worry and what-ifs often consumed her, but she'd already committed to acting as Denzin's girlfriend in public. What harm would come from messing around?

It might make their act more convincing. Or make returning to work miserable.

She took a deep breath and released it slowly before pulling on a bra, underwear, and a slip. Before she slid into her dress, she needed a few of the toiletries she'd stored in the bathroom. She could wait—*or* she could use it as an excuse to be in the same room as Denzin while *he* was naked in the shower. Her pulse sped at the thought.

He'd been present for most of her shower. It could be a thing between them now. Only seemed fair.

Toni tapped on the door as the loud spray of water stopped. "Can I come in and get my cosmetic bag?"

Denzin let out a gruff, "Come in," and she entered. He wore a chalet towel around his waist. Toni's towel had barely reached around her body. On him it appeared tiny—and it immediately slid from his hips and fell to the ground.

She froze midway to the counter as she took him in. Yeti were covered head to toe in white fur and biologically designed to be without clothes. Supposedly, when aroused, a yeti's dick would emerge from their sheath. But fur obscured their sheath. Toni knew. She'd seen naked yeti—Rabten was comfortable without clothes, and she'd even glimpsed Denzin naked once, years ago from afar. She'd looked for his mysterious sheath but hadn't seen it. Tonight she fought to keep her gaze above his waist and lost—but still couldn't make it out.

She gnawed at her lower lip as she raised her gaze. Denzin's eyes had narrowed, and he openly looked up and down her body. So hot to see the normally disciplined manager break the rules. Although she might be attempting to forget her fears and live for the moment, Toni needed to ease into it.

She didn't even remember what she'd come in for. "I, um, need lip gloss," she mumbled before shoving a hand into her bag, while Denzin retrieved his towel from the floor.

Her wet hair needed product, drying, and styling, and she hadn't yet applied makeup. But she only grabbed the lip gloss before quickly fleeing, leaving Denzin on his own.

He exited a short time later. While he dressed, she did her hair and makeup in the bathroom. Still in her slip, she came out to find him buttoning a charcoal-gray suit.

God he knew how to dress. Her mouth watered at the sight of him.

Adjusting his cuffs, Denzin turned, his blue eyes devouring her. Her nipples went rock hard. Again. If the quirk of his lips was any indication, he'd noticed. "Are you wearing the dress with the flower pattern this evening? It's hanging in the closet. I thought this suit would best match."

Her breath caught. He'd color coordinated for her. "You brought more than one suit?"

He nodded and simply said, "I didn't know what you'd be wearing." He held a tie in each hand. "Burgundy or navy?"

Toni strode to his accessories and selected a bright blue tie. "How about this one? It'll match my dress and bring out your eyes."

Said eyes held hers while he wrapped and knotted the cloth around his neck. Her pulse quickened and blood rushed through her veins. He lifted his arms as if for her inspection.

She hummed appreciatively. "You look very handsome, Denzin. You always do, but especially tonight."

He didn't respond but she swore a low growl sounded from his chest as she moved to the closet. She slipped the dress off the hanger and carefully stepped into it, pulling it up her body. When she reached back for the zipper, large hands met hers.

"Let me."

She swallowed—hard—and scooped her hair out of the way.

His hands brushed her lower back as he grasped the zipper. He slid it up, his touch lingering on the back of her neck, his warm fingers heating her skin.

When he stepped away she glanced up at him through her lashes. "Thank you," she said before raising her arms in the same fashion as he had, slowly spinning so he could appraise her front and back.

He sexy-growled his approval. "You will undoubtedly be the most beautiful woman at the wedding."

She grinned, wanting more of this side of Denzin. "More beautiful than the bride?"

He blinked, his face growing serious. "No contest. There never has been where you're concerned."

What exactly did he mean by that? She wasn't sure, but her body liked those words. Her heart struck a faster rhythm as he held up her jacket, and she slipped her arms into her sleeves.

They put on their winter boots for the snowy walk to the chalet. Denzin, carrying a bag with her heels and his dress shoes, offered her his arm. The perfect escort through the winter night.

Toni had never arrived at an event feeling so beautiful or special. As she and Denzin stepped into the chalet, it seemed like they might steal the show from the bride and groom.

Denzin paused as they crossed the threshold and turned, his breath warm against her neck as he whispered, "You ready for this?"

She regarded him with a smile and nod. Oh yes, Toni was ready.

His focus shifted to her lips, now fully glossed. Warmth spread through her as his hand settled on the small of her back, and he guided her toward her ogling mother. In a low voice, he rumbled, "Me too."

CHAPTER FIVE

Denzin had never felt more alive as he escorted Toni to a tall bar table where Bev and Mari's mother, Anne, had their heads bent together in conversation. "Ladies," he said, nodding as they approached. "You both look lovely this evening."

"And you two make a very striking couple," Anne said.

Denzin's chest swelled at her compliment, and when Toni beamed and placed a hand on his chest, his sense of confidence and well-being skyrocketed. No, he and Toni hadn't kissed—yet—but flirting was wicked fun, and they had the whole weekend ahead of them.

It felt natural to slide his hand around Toni's hip

and pull her closer. She leaned into him like she belonged there, and he loved the feel of her against his body, his palm splayed across her side. He didn't have to try to act normal. Holding her this way felt natural.

Mari and Pema approached. Mari's eyes sparkled as she regarded them. Pema's mouth hung open. Mari nudged her with an elbow, and Pema quickly clamped her azure lips around a cocktail straw. She looked about, as if taking in everyone else's reaction to Denzin and Toni.

Denzin addressed the small group. "Can I get anyone a drink?" He turned to Toni. "White wine for you, unless they only have chardonnay?" He knew she preferred white but thought chardonnay tasted like canned corn.

Her lips lifted into a pleased smile that made him ridiculously happy. "Yes, thank you."

He took three orders and headed to the bar tended by Mari's younger sister. When he returned with the drinks, Bev sipped her spritzer and asked, "So, how long have you been dating my daughter?"

Denzin felt all eyes on him, including Toni's, but smoothly replied, "Since this summer, but who can pinpoint an exact date on something like that?"

Bev didn't look happy. "Any woman could give

an exact date. It will be one of your anniversaries. You'll need to send Toni flowers." Denzin pictured a bouquet of wild iris rather than the tropical arrangement Toni had fictitiously described to Julia earlier.

"Mom, every relationship is unique. Stop nagging my boyfriend."

Boyfriend. That's a title I want for real. He suppressed a pleased grin and rubbed small circles across Toni's shoulder blades in a show of support. Had he ever been anyone's boyfriend? Julia had never referred to him as such. Mostly he'd had flings or casual relationships, and those were few and far between. Yeti had small social circles.

Anne frowned. "I thought you two started dating last New Year's Eve. That's what Mari and Tseten told me."

Mari pressed her lips together, while Pema tried to cover a snort-laugh with a cough, then went to work again on her cocktail straw.

Tseten walked up. "Did I hear my name?"

"I thought you said these two got together last New Year's. Rang in midnight with a big old smooch," Anne said.

Denzin paused, his drink at his lips. Kiss? Not *the* kiss? Had they noticed it after all? And if everyone else noticed the kiss, had it also affected Toni as much as it had affected him?

She distracted him by sliding her arm around his middle, her warm hand between his jacket and shirt. *Gods, that feels good.*

"See, Mom," she said. "It's been gradual. We don't have a dating anniversary."

Denzin ran his fingers down Toni's arm and added, "And I don't need a reason to send Toni flowers."

He couldn't deny that the chorus of "awws" around the table pleased him—enough that the approaching bride didn't affect him like she might have. At least not immediately.

"What are we oohing and aahing about?" Julia asked.

Tseten nodded in Denzin's direction. "Mr. Romantic over here."

Despite Tseten's gesture, Julia glanced around the entire group before her sights landed on him. "Denzin? A romantic?" She snickered.

Denzin inwardly sighed, but then Toni threaded her fingers through his, physically linking herself to him in front of everyone.

"What can I say," Toni retorted. "I must bring out the best in him."

He squeezed Toni's hand. *Perfection.*

"Well, whatever," Julia laughed. It looked forced, but he couldn't quite bring himself to feel bad for her. "I need to borrow *Mr. Romantic,*" she said, using air quotes for fuck's sake, "for the rehearsal."

Determined to take the higher ground, Denzin placed a kiss on Toni's knuckles, which had gone white, she gripped him so tightly while her eyes shot daggers at Julia. "If you'll excuse me," he said to their companions. To Toni, he added, "I'll meet up with you for dinner."

As he followed Julia through the chalet, she went on about all the places Wes planned to take her after the wedding. Denzin was about to respond along the lines of, "You're very fortunate," when Wes walked up and pulled her away, albeit still within earshot.

"Baby, why are you telling Denzin all this?"

"He's family, or will be, and he can't travel."

Wes let out a sigh. "It might come across as if you're pointing out all the things he can't do."

Denzin tried not to look too exasperated as they talked about the giant yeti in the room as if he wasn't there.

"Okay, well, sorry to share our good news, or whatever," Julia said to Denzin after she returned to his side. She didn't have much experience with apologies. "About the ceremony," she continued. "I'm thinking that this chair arrangement is all wrong. Why don't you come in the morning and line these chairs up the other way?"

Denzin was done playing errand boy. "No."

She stared at him blankly, like she couldn't believe he'd refused. "Why ever not?"

He had the urge to tell her he'd be too busy making love to Toni, bringing her to orgasm half a dozen times before he performed their wedding, and therefore wouldn't have time. But he would never say that, and instead responded, "I'm going hiking. Not that it's any of your business. I'm sure there are others who could help rearrange the seating."

He had no plans to hike, but he and his friends regularly enjoyed the activity, and the trails that led from the chalet to the surrounding peaks were spectacular, even in winter. Saying no and telling Julia that his plans, his life, were none of her business seemed to startle her into a stunned silence that continued as the others arrived for the short ceremony rehearsal.

As soon as they finished, Denzin quickly sought Tseten to corroborate a group hike plan for the morning. Then he returned to the bar for another old fashioned and a glass of wine for Toni. He had the feeling it would be a long night, and they'd both need the extra fortification.

TONI SWIRLED her wine before taking a large gulp. The New Year's Eve kiss. A heinous bride. And questions. Lots and lots of questions. At least her knuckles still tingled from the sweet brush of Denzin's lips.

Toni had been obsessing over that New Year's kiss for nearly a year. But she never imagined her friends had noticed it. She'd been more preoccupied with its significance to Denzin—and herself. She should ask him about it . . . Maybe after more wine.

"I just realized," Anne said to Toni and Mari. "You two are the same age now as Bev and I when we were both pregnant with you. We first met in our birthing class."

Good god. Not the "When are you going to have kids?" talk. Toni exchanged a glance with Mari, and they both drained their glasses.

Mari pinched the bridge of her nose. "Mom, why would you bring that up?"

"What's the problem? I look at you girls, and you

remind me of us at your age. But we were both mothers already—to you two."

"And had a lot more responsibilities," Toni's mother added unhelpfully. "And since we're on the topic of children. Just remember that there's never a right time to plan for a family."

"Mom!" Toni cried, "Don't even go there."

"What? I won't say anything in front of Denzin —unless he's open to it. But you're not young forever. You need to keep that in mind. Plan for it like you do your professional career."

It was possible a vein burst in Toni's temple. "I can't even—" she began, before being interrupted by an announcement to move into the dining room.

Mari pulled Toni aside, lips pursed as if smothering a smile. "You and Denzin are sitting with our mothers. My seat is across the room with my dates."

"What? No!" Toni gave her a horrified look. "Don't abandon me," she hissed over the noise of the crowd. The collective volume had grown with the consumption of alcohol at the open bar.

Mari waggled her fingers goodbye as she mouthed, "Sorry, not sorry," and backed away to find Tseten and Pema.

Toni rounded on the two older women. "No more talk about children. If I ever decide to start a family, I will tell you—same goes for Mari. Until then, no hints or questions. Agreed?"

Her mother rolled her eyes. "You're being overly sensitive."

Toni crossed her arms. "I'm not."

Anne gave Toni's arm a squeeze, then glanced at Toni's mother as if looking for consensus. "You're right, dear. It's none of our business."

Her mother neither agreed nor disagreed. "We're only looking out for your well-being."

"Thank you. I think," Toni said, not quite trusting her mother.

As much as the relationship questions and not-so-subtle biological clock reminders annoyed Toni, her mother and Anne meant well. The older Toni became, the more she recognized the hardships her mother endured when her father had died. Not only had she lost the love of her life, but she'd also changed careers so she could afford the mortgage, allowing them to stay in Wildwood until Toni finished high school.

Eventually, they made it to their table, and Anne excused herself to say hello to a friend. Toni sat across from her mother and helped herself to one of the two bottles of wine placed near their settings. She sloshed wine when her mother gasped.

"I've just remembered," her mother said. "You went on a date when you came to visit me over Valentine's Day."

Toni nearly gagged at the creamed corn taste of an oaky chardonnay, but that didn't stop her from taking a second sip. "So?"

"So?" Her mother's eyes nearly bugged out of her head. "You need to tell Denzin."

A fresh glass of wine appeared before Toni, and calloused fingers glided across her shoulder. She didn't have to fake a pleased smile at his return.

"Tell me what?" Denzin asked as he took the seat next to her.

Toni resisted rolling her eyes. "I had a blind date last February when I visited my mom in Seattle."

She expected him to grin or nudge her shoulder and share a quiet laugh at her mother's ridiculousness. Instead, the happy creases at the corner of his eyes faded. "After New Year's," he confirmed, as if giving the events and the timing more consideration.

Toni's annoyance and the subtle humor in the situation fled. The others around them seemed to fade as Denzin became her entire focus. Six weeks after their kiss, she'd gone on a blind date. He realized her position, didn't he? He'd hired her in January. She couldn't chase after him. She worked for him and had her reputation to consider as a small business owner. Plus, he knew her mother. "My mom set me up."

Denzin's deep blue gaze didn't waver from hers. "I can imagine. Did you . . . enjoy yourself?"

She blinked, the truth spilling from her lips. "I spent the evening comparing my date to you."

His eyes softened, and she swallowed hard. Why hadn't she made something up? Was the truth too much?

"Well," her mother said, breaking the silence. "I hope you can forgive my daughter, Denzin."

He covered Toni's hand with his own and gave her mother a reassuring smile. "There's nothing to forgive. As we've said, our relationship has developed over time."

Denzin's words and the weight of his hand on hers made Toni's heart flop wildly in her chest.

"We're sitting next to Toni and Denzin," a female voice said from behind Toni. She looked up as Helen and Rabten pulled out the chairs next to her.

Where Denzin had closely cut his facial fur, Rab wore his much longer, though he appeared well groomed for the evening, even if he'd opted for jeans and a button-up shirt. But "dressing up" in Alaska had many definitions, as seen by Helen's cute sweater and flowy skirt. Given their matching smiles and hand-holding, they looked every bit a happy couple. Helen had supposedly moved back to Alaska for Rab.

"You guys made it," Toni said as she and Denzin both stood to greet them.

Denzin clapped Rab on the back and to Helen said, "Glad you've extended your time in Alaska and could join us after all."

Helen wrapped her arms around Rab and kissed his cheek. "Me too."

For a moment, Rab only seemed to have eyes for Helen. Then he added to the group, "We almost didn't make it tonight. It's been storm after storm this winter, but Dale managed to fly out and pick us up."

Toni addressed her mother. "Mom, you remember Rabten, don't you?"

Her mother smiled. "Of course. You must still be caretaking at Toklat Lodge." She placed a hand on her chest. "Those rooms and that view—it's one of my favorite places in Alaska."

All agreed before Toni made further introductions. "And this is Helen, Rab's girlfriend."

Her mother's eyes shone. "Girlfriend," she

repeated with a smile. "Tell me, how did you two meet? How long have you been together?"

A fleeting moment of guilt washed over Toni at having her mother's relationship preoccupation shift to other people. But she needed the breathing room. They all sat, and Toni scooped up the wine glass that Denzin had brought her as Helen and Rab answered her mother's rapid-fire questions.

Denzin leaned in and clicked his cocktail glass to hers. "To less drama in the second half of this evening," he said in a low voice.

"Was Julia that bad?" Toni already knew the answer.

Denzin shrugged and took a large sip from his tumbler. "We're hiking in the morning, by the way. If you have enough warm gear."

"Hiking?"

"I needed an excuse to get out of chair rearrangement." He grimaced then in a low voice admitted, "I didn't need an excuse, but I was compelled to give one."

Before she realized what she was doing, Toni placed a hand on his knee. The move felt as natural as his hand on hers a moment ago. "Then we hike. I have long underwear and snow pants," she confirmed before one of her mother's questions caught her attention.

"And did you know about my daughter and Denzin?" her mother asked Rab and Helen.

Panic flared. Had anyone told them about their fake dating arrangement? *How much do they know?*

With a grin and a wink, Helen said, "These two have chemistry. I picked up on it over Halloween in Denali."

Had she really sensed chemistry a few weeks ago? Toni didn't have time to ponder. They needed this to stop. "I'm sure Rab and Helen don't want to talk about us. Let's guess what's on the buffet tonight. Smells great. Maybe meatballs?" She glanced around the table, hoping for some participation in changing the subject, but her mother still held Rab's focus.

"Before Halloween," Rab added. "I thought they got together at New Year's."

Toni's breath caught. They'd all seen the New Year's Eve kiss? She nudged Denzin.

He gave her a questioning look, then added, "The program said they're serving two entrees, rockfish or meatballs. Good guess."

The others ignored them.

Her mother asked, "*Got together*. What does that mean?"

Rab stiffened. "You'll have to ask them."

"Rockfish is my favorite," Toni exclaimed. "Mom, you love rockfish."

Her mother frowned. "Yes, it's generally better than dried-out halibut. But Toni, you're trying to change the subject. You didn't tell me you and Denzin were dating, and I'm curious if all your friends knew."

Denzin slid his arm around Toni, the heat of him surrounding her. "I can answer that for you, Bev." His voice was deep, rumbly, and authoritative as he pulled Toni snug against his massive body. The show of possession frankly made her panties wet. "They didn't know. We only told you, Mari, and Tseten yesterday."

Soft lips whispered a kiss against her cheek, sending a thrill through Toni's body. She had to be blushing from head to toe, but didn't much care at the moment. Not with Denzin larger than life behind her.

Denzin turned to Helen and Rab and announced, "Toni and I are dating, if you hadn't heard."

They appeared nonplussed. Did they already

assume the two were in a relationship? She and Denzin could tell them the truth later.

"That's wonderful," Helen finally said with a genuine smile that made Toni a little sad. *If only this could be real.*

After a subtle nudge from Helen, Rab lifted his drink. "Cheers. I'm happy for you."

Denzin then turned back to Toni's mother. "Bev, we'll answer whatever questions you have. Ask away."

Toni jerked against Denzin. *No!* When offered an inch her mother took a mile. "Mom, he didn't mean that *everything* was open for discussion."

Bev smiled like a cat with cream and propped her elbows on the table. She ignored Toni. "Thank you for that offer, Denzin. Tell me. Do you want children?"

Ah, geez . . .

But without missing a beat, Denzin said, "Yes . . . when the time is right."

Toni nearly choked on her wine because of the ease of his answer and because, well, Denzin wanted kids. A million thoughts spun through her head as she analyzed what that meant and how she might or might not fit into that scenario. Did she want to? Would she ever feel like she could?

Helen stood. "They've called our table for dinner." She flashed a knowing smile at Toni. "Let's get some rockfish before it's gone."

Toni owed Helen—big time. "Excellent idea." Toni shot to her feet, tugging Denzin up with her, and effectively shutting down her mother's questioning, at least for now.

So far, nothing about this weekend had gone as she'd imagined. Too early to determine if that was good, bad, or disastrous.

CHAPTER SIX

D enzin leaned on the table, his chin resting in his palm and an undoubtedly sappy smile pasted on his face. He'd never heard Toni giggle so much. It amused his not-quite-sober self.

She collapsed against him in a fit of laughter, reacting to something Mari said. It gave him an excuse to drape his arm around her shoulders. He didn't care that the crowd had thinned, and they didn't need to pretend in front of their friends. They'd been touching each other all night, and now Denzin couldn't—no, didn't want to—keep his hands off her.

Tseten pulled out his phone. If he had judgmental thoughts about Denzin and Toni, they weren't obvious. "So we're hiking in the morning?"

Denzin nodded. "We can hike partway up Polaris Peak. The trail starts behind the cabins. We don't have to go far."

Tseten gave him a knowing look. "Far enough to not be available for the bride's last-minute task list."

Denzin shrugged and drained his water. He didn't want to talk about his soon-to-be sister-in-law and how she treated him. "That's the plan."

"Alright, then I'm going to bed now," Tseten said. He turned to his platonic dates. "Ladies, are you ready? Can I escort you to our room?"

Toni let out a chuckle. "Are you all in the same room?"

Mari leaned back in her chair, a teasing grin on her face. "It's not bad. Pema and I are sharing one bed, and Tset's in the other. He's promised to wear his nose strip and not talk about Rosa in his dreams."

Tseten rolled his eyes while the others snickered. "Let's go, musketeers. I think you two need a chaperone. Also, I don't snore."

Thankfully, they hadn't questioned his and Toni's sleeping arrangement in their secluded cabin.

Toni surveyed the now empty room. "I think the party is over."

Denzin smiled at her. "Shall we return to our cabin?"

She gave an eager nod. "God yes." After draining her water, Denzin helped her to her feet. A bit unsteady—they'd both had too much to drink—she wobbled, then took his arm, one he gladly offered. He seized the moment, pulling her close as they walked to the coat closet.

"Is it just me, or is it harder to walk now than before dinner?" Toni questioned.

"Should we blame the fish?" He deadpanned before leaning her against the doorframe as he collected their winter gear.

She huffed a laugh. "Either the fish or the wine. Might never know." When he returned to her side, she balanced against him while attempting to slip her feet into her boots. "No, really"—she giggled—"I can do this."

"Let me help." He sat her in a chair. The laces on her boots were knotted. "How did you . . ." He scratched his head. They didn't need to deal with this tonight. Denzin helped her back into her heels.

"What are you doing?" she asked. "I can't trudge through the snow with these on."

"You won't have to," he murmured while he put her boots and his dress shoes in their bag. He shouldered it, then leaned down and scooped her into his arms, bride style. She let out a whoop of laughter before muffling the rest into his chest.

"Zin, I can untie the laces and put my boots on." Her breath was warm, hot even, against his neck as she spoke. The sensation thrilled him.

"In the morning," he said, as they exited through the front door and out into the snowy night.

"No one has ever carried me before," she admitted. "Not like this anyway."

He glanced down to find her looking up at him. "I've never carried anyone." But she felt good in his arms. Like she was meant to be there.

They walked in silence, the crunch of snow the only sound in the quiet night as Toni burrowed into him. He could get used to this, her closeness and subtle floral scent surrounding him.

Outside the cabin, she let out a small gasp. "Shooting star."

He tracked the night sky at the end of her finger to see the fiery tail disappear over the dark mountain ridge. "Did you make a wish?" he asked as he opened their door and carried her inside.

Toni shifted in his arms as he set her down. Instead of moving away, she turned into him, her body and all her curves slowly sliding along his until her feet hit the floor. She looked up into his eyes, arms still looped around his neck. "Yes. Did you?"

He'd wished to make this charade with Toni the real thing. It felt pretty fucking real.

She blinked up at him. "You kissed me on New Year's Eve."

Denzin's breath caught. *The kiss.* When he could breathe again he said, "You kissed me back."

"Yeah." Her gaze darted to his mouth. "I did."

A beat passed as they held each other, her words sinking in. *I didn't imagine those sweet lips moving against mine.*

"We should try it again," Toni whispered. "You've seen me naked now. We might be doing things out of order."

Denzin's arms tightened around her, a growl building in his chest as he thought back to seeing Toni in the shower earlier. Toni, glowing skin beaded with water. She'd seen him naked too, though he had a lot less to hide at the time.

"I'd like that," he rumbled. But as he lowered his head, they swayed, and he paused. An open bar had made it too simple to ease tension with alcohol. Gods, Toni's mother had asked him if he wanted children, and Julia complained to him about the flowers—as if by transporting them he was somehow responsible for the high percentage of filler flowers in the arrangements.

He searched Toni's half-lidded eyes. "I want to kiss you, but we've had too much to drink. Let's revisit this tomorrow when our heads are clear?"

She drew her bottom lip between her teeth, and Denzin nearly groaned with need. She nodded and slowly untwined her arms, but her forehead creased. "You're still going to sleep with me, aren't you?" A sweet smile spread across her face. "I mean, sleep in the same bed as me?"

He wanted nothing more than to tuck under the covers with Toni. "It's big enough that we can stick to our own sides." And he would respect her space, her person.

"You're very thoughtful, Denzin," she commented before helping him out of his jacket.

A moment later he untangled her arms from her dress after she pulled it over her head. Undressing each other tonight wasn't sexy, but comfortable, and a new level of intimacy. He stopped at his boxers and stepped into the bathroom as Toni wriggled into her pajamas.

"Don't laugh," she called to him. "I didn't think we'd be staying together when I packed."

If she wanted him to not laugh, she couldn't be

wearing a sexy nightie—he didn't imagine her for the type, anyway. He tore off a strand of dental floss, then came out to look.

She wore a patterned night shirt and shorts. Adorable. She held up the hem of the shirt for his inspection, a blush creeping across her cheeks. "They're little yeti."

He touched the tip of her nose with his finger. "I approve." He wanted to ask if she thought of him when she wore them, but what if the answer was no? Instead, he handed her the dental floss.

She looked at the container in her palm. "You floss?"

He wound the strand between his fingers. "Don't you?"

Her blush deepened. "Yes, of course." But she paused before shaking her head. "Actually, I'm terrible at remembering to floss." She broke off a length. "Thank you."

She followed him into the bathroom, glancing at his toothpaste tube. "I like spearmint," she shared. "Do you have a favorite?"

He liked getting to know Toni on this level. He finished flossing and grabbed his toothbrush. "I know I don't like bacon flavor." He wetted the brush and explained, "It was a gag gift from Tseten."

She made a face. "Gross. I mean, don't get me wrong, I like bacon with almost anything, but not foaming in my mouth."

After they both finished in the bathroom, they approached the bed, and Denzin drew back the covers. "Do you want the wall or the edge?"

She bounced onto the mattress. "Sleeping between the wall and a yeti sounds cozy."

He wanted to wrap her in his big, furry arms and teach her the true definition of cozy. Instead, he climbed into bed after her, careful to stay on his own side. The mattress groaned under his weight, and he reached to switch off the light. "Sleep well, Antoinette."

"Mmm . . ." she responded, as she squirmed and snuggled in. "Sweet dreams, Denzin."

Not too sweet, he hoped, or he'd wake up with a raging hard-on, and there would be no hiding the topic of his dreams. He pictured those lovely breasts he'd seen in the shower earlier and what might happen when they woke up sober.

They laid in silence for several minutes before the back of her hand brushed his, her fingers gently entwining with his large digits. While his heart hammered, she remained still, her breath growing deep, steady on the other side of the bed.

Eventually, sleep overtook Denzin, and he drifted off, hand in hand with Toni.

TONI KNEW EXACTLY where she was when she woke up on the day of the wedding—on top of Denzin. It thrilled her as much as it scared her.

She didn't experience a groggy "where am I" moment. The instant sleep faded, she recognized she lay upon a hot, furry, muscular mass—her bed partner and date for the weekend. He was also her boss, but she pushed that reality from her mind.

Instead of jumping back or rolling off him, Toni focused on all the sensations of Denzin's body against hers. Heat radiated off him like an electric blanket. The soft fur of his chest tickled and caressed her cheek and the palm of her splayed hand. And her sex throbbed where it pressed into his massive thigh, wedged between her spread legs.

But she still didn't move, not even when her nipples puckered and the hair on her arms lifted. She could hardly resist the urge to grind and rub herself against him, or run her hand down his chest and under the blankets in discovery. What did the mysterious yeti sheath look like? Feel like? More to the point, what did Denzin's look and feel like?

Toni gently turned her head to look up at his sleeping face. Long, white eyelashes rested against the blue skin of his cheeks. His face appeared relaxed, vulnerable even.

Lashes fluttered, and his breathing altered slightly. "Good morning, Antoinette," he rumbled.

The vibrations of his voice hardened her nipples into solid points that happily pressed into his chest. Could he feel them? "Morning," she returned, her voice coming out in a breathy pant.

Denzin's arm tightened around her, his fingers finding a gap between her pajama top and bottom. His soft palm and the fur on his wrist tickled her bare skin. He bent his fingers and his blunt claws lightly raked across her hip and lower back.

She shivered under his touch, his name rushing out in a whoosh of breath.

He growled in return, his chest reverberating. His slitted eyes fixed on hers. His other arm came around her back, sliding her up his chest until their faces were level.

Toni blinked, her mouth mere inches from Denzin's. She focused solely on this moment, not her worries, not her preoccupations with their professional relationship or what others thought. Just him and her, and the chemistry that caused the air around them to sizzle.

She was in bed with Denzin, his powerful arms locking her to his body, her legs spread wide across his torso. Toni wanted to give in to her urges, act on her feelings.

"We're sober now," she observed, her gaze sliding to Denzin's lush, cerulean lips.

"We are," he replied, his husky voice causing her skin to heat. "Are you suggesting something, Antoinette?"

She swallowed then went for it, her words escaping in a husky rush. "I want you, Denzin."

His eyes flared a brighter blue than she'd ever seen. He growled again, a primal, but pleased, sound. "I want you too. Badly."

She shivered in anticipation. The small drawer full of giant condoms was only an arm's reach away.

She lowered her face, only closing her eyes when her lips touched his. They set a slow pace, exploring each other, teasing. Toni ran her tongue along his lower lip. His chest vibrated in response, and he tightened his hold. He let her explore his mouth before his tongue met hers.

Their kiss deepened, and Toni ran her hands

along the sides of his face, wanting more of him. His short beard lightly scraped her palms, and her hips ground into him of their own accord.

Denzin growled again, the hand under her shirt slid up her back, claws grazing her skin. His other hand cupped her ass. She moaned her approval, craving his touch. He responded, and her body gave a jolt when his fingers curved around and brushed against her core.

"You're wet," he ground out. "Soaked through your panties and pajamas."

"I'm not wearing panties."

He grunted, fingers pressing harder against her throbbing center. "I would rip these bottoms right off you if they weren't covered in yeti. If you want this, then pants off, Toni. Now."

Yes. Yes, she wanted everything very badly. To feel him against her and not through a damp piece of flannel. Toni shimmied out of her pajama bottoms as quickly as she could.

Denzin pulled her back on top of him. "Hold on to the bed frame—both hands."

Tentatively, she leaned forward, her bare thighs shaking as she realized what he intended. They skipped straight from kissing to third base—or was oral a homerun? She didn't really care as he gripped her legs and moved himself lower until his large, furry face was directly under her drenched pussy. *Oh god.* She whimpered his name.

Full, wet lips trailed kisses along her inner thighs, preparing her for the even more intimate touches to come. He parted her with his fingers. "So fucking beautiful," he rumbled.

She looked down to watch him, his entire focus between her legs. His eyes met hers, and he swiped a textured, blue tongue from her entrance to her clit. A cry ripped from her throat.

"You like that, Antoinette? You taste fucking amazing."

She moaned above him, her hips jerking. She moved against his tongue as he lapped at her entrance and flicked against her swollen bundle of nerves. "You feel incredible."

He doubled down at her praise, his tongue moving faster against her. Beads of sweat pricked her forehead. She had to stop herself from grinding down onto him.

When she thought she couldn't bear much more, his pace slowed. He licked his way to her entrance before dipping inside of her. She released a strangled moan at the sensation of his thick, velvety, yeti tongue sliding in and out of her. He adjusted his hand, his large thumb swirling through her wetness before centering on her clit.

"Zin, yes, please." Pleasure grew, nearly overwhelming her. Like riding a wave that threatened to crest but kept building instead. When she finally tipped over the edge, her whole body shook with release, her channel clenched around his tongue. Her hips moved against his finger until she became too sensitive and jerked away.

Toni collapsed on the bed next to Denzin. He scooted up, and she moved down until her lips found his. She might have morning breath, but he tasted of her musky scent. He kissed her with an enthusiasm that showed he didn't care. Their lips mashed, tongues tangled, and Toni's hand traveled down Denzin's body. She palmed the large bulge in his boxer briefs.

She finally had her chance and would not chicken out. "I want to see you," she demanded. "Now."

A THRILL RACED through Denzin at Toni's words, her exacting tone. He wanted nothing more than to show her how hard he'd become while licking her sweet pussy.

She broke away from his embrace, shoving down the covers to reveal his body. She slid eager hands into the waistband of his boxers, and he helped her pull them down.

Toni gasped as his thick, blue cock bobbed against his taut, furry stomach. "Oh my."

He reached down and stroked himself. "That's why the condoms are extra, extra-large."

"Can I touch you? Taste you?"

Denzin's lids lowered halfway, and he nodded. "Please." He wouldn't deny her anything, and he ached for her touch.

Wandering hands moved between his legs, her fingers tracking over the furry area at the base of his dick, setting off sparks of pleasure. "This is your mysterious sheath?"

In a breathy grunt, he repeated, "Mysterious?"

"It holds a hell of a lot of cock for something that isn't visible under your fur when you're naked."

He chuckled. "It swells and engorges, like a human dick, then drops from the sheath."

"Ooh," she responded with a mischievous smirk. "Talk science to me." She moved her hands, her fingers ghosting over the sensitive skin of his shaft.

Denzin squirmed. "Play fair. No tickling."

She encircled his dick in a firm grip and ran her hands up and down his length. Her touch made his eyelids flutter and a vibrating growl build in his chest. When a bead of liquid formed at the tip of his cock, Toni leaned forward and slowly licked it off before taking his crown into her mouth.

Watching his blue dick slide between her plump, pink lips made him even harder. And when the tip hit the back of her throat, he nearly came. He reached for her, wanting to both touch her and needing to grab at something to stop himself from flipping her over and burying himself in her sweetness. "Gods, Toni," he muttered.

With her lips tight around him, she moved her mouth and hands up and down his shaft, head bobbing as she alternated her speed. He couldn't stop the moans of pleasure as she worked him.

Eventually, it all became too much. With his free hand, he fisted the sheets, trying to control his urge to thrust into her as his balls tightened. "Mmm . . . Toni, I'm going to come." He wanted to give her the option of removing her mouth. He also fleetingly thought about the condoms, but yeti dick was big, and he'd need to prepare Toni. They'd have time for that later.

Toni, mouth open wide around his thickness, only worked him harder, twisting her hands along his length to bring him to his climax.

He leaned up and cupped the back of her head as he released into her eager mouth. Chest heaving, he let out a deep growl of satisfaction.

Toni swallowed and eased her grip. Her mouth was still on his cock, and Denzin's gaze locked with hers, his breath coming in harsh pants. Gods, he wanted this woman.

As soon as she popped her lips off his tip, he lifted her into his lap. His mouth devoured hers, his tongue thrusting into her in a rhythm he hoped to match later with his dick. She met his frenzied kiss, her tongue sliding against his, her hands roaming his body.

"Worth waiting for a sober kiss." She gasped as he licked his way down her neck to her chest.

He growled in return. "So worth it."

Denzin's lips were about to close around the tight swollen bud of Toni's nipple when a loud knock sounded at the door, they froze, their breaths coming rapidly, chests heaving in their passion.

Tseten's all too cheerful voice boomed, "This is your wake-up call."

"And coffee delivery," Mari added.

Toni snagged her plump lip with her teeth. Was she worried about them finding out what they'd just done?

"They don't have to know," Denzin assured her, concerned that she might have doubts. "You hit the shower. I'll deal with these guys."

She gave a nod.

"We woke up late. Be right there," he yelled.

He followed Toni into the bathroom and quickly rinsed her sweet, musky scent off his face—other yeti would notice it.

Toni grabbed his hand and pulled him down for another kiss. "I'm not finished. I want you inside of me—and not only my mouth. I want it all."

Sweet summer snow.

Denzin groaned. "Tonight?"

She nodded, a slow smile spreading across her face. "After the wedding."

He placed a quick kiss on her swollen lips. "I'll be looking forward to it all day."

More like obsessing.

CHAPTER SEVEN

Toni's girly bits were still singing the sweet praises of Denzin's skillful tongue throughout their hike. Maybe they could get in a quickie before the ceremony. And then more sex after.

But as they neared the Aurora cabin on their return, Mari asked, "You're getting ready with me and Pema, right, Toni? I'm doing makeup, and Pema's on hair." She paused and waggled her eyebrows. "Or does Denzin need help with his tuxedo zipper?" She cracked up at her own joke.

Toni glanced back at Denzin. He and Tseten walked a few paces behind. "I'm pretty adept at my own fly," he said dryly.

Toni had been looking forward to dressing for the wedding with him. She couldn't wait for the sexy times to come, but also craved the small, domestic tasks like helping him with his bowtie. She forbade herself to continue thinking past this weekend or to doubt what she and Denzin were doing. So far, it all felt right. Right and so, so good. And though she'd convinced herself that she and Denzin could still have sex and fake date, she didn't want to give her friends any reason to question the status of their relationship. Plus, she didn't want to ditch her girlfriends, and it would be fun to dress and primp with them.

"Yes, I'd still like to get ready with you guys," she finally responded. "I'll grab my things as we pass by the cabin."

Pema grinned. "Excellent. We can have the room to ourselves since Tset agreed to rush through his grooming. I mean, what does he really need to do?"

Tseten rolled his eyes. "Just give me ten minutes in the bathroom," he said. "Then I'll head to the bar." He turned to Denzin. "Do you have any special officiant duties?"

"Aside from performing the ceremony and moving chairs for Julia? I hope not." He let out a harsh laugh. "Thanks for getting me out of chair duty."

Mari, cheeks flushed from their walk, turned and

said, "The hike also got me out of a chat with Nima's mother, so thanks. She needs to talk to her son, not his . . . ex."

No one knew why Nima and Mari broke up. They'd traveled together to the Sierra Nevada Range in California, but Mari had returned alone on a plane, unwilling to answer questions.

Toni attempted to lighten the conversation. "Another bonus of this walk? We all exercised before eating wedding pie."

Mari came to a full stop. "Wait. We *are* having pie, right? If Julia pulls some kind of pumpkin wedding cake shit after hijacking our Thanksgiving holiday, I'm gonna have words." She looked around. "Well, words for someone. Likely you guys. I won't ruin Julia's day. But I'll make my own damn pie later this weekend."

Tseten raised a hand. "Text me for that."

They arrived at the cabin. After twenty-four hours at the chalet, Toni now realized it was referred to as *secluded* because it was the farthest from the chalet. Julia had frosted over the part where she'd given her ex, and soon-to-be brother-in-law, the longest walk through the snow to the festivities.

"I'll only be a minute," Toni called to her friends

as she and Denzin entered the cabin. Tseten hurried ahead to take his shower.

Toni grabbed her toiletry bag from the bathroom. Denzin followed her in, and when she turned and saw the blazing hunger in his eyes, she stopped dead in her tracks. A thrill streaked through her body—from a *look*. They weren't even touching. "I wanted to get ready with you," she admitted.

He responded with a low growl. "Then I better give you something to think about while you're with them."

Her bag landed on the counter with a thud before she launched herself into Denzin's ready arms, their lips connecting in a scorching kiss. *God, yes.* Couldn't they stay in and do this all afternoon?

She forced herself to pull back. "I appreciate that. And I want you to know . . . you, and what we'll do later tonight, are the only things on my mind."

Denzin pressed his forehead against hers, his hands moving to her hips. "Same." He gave her one last brush of his lips before handing her the toiletry bag.

Toni collected her dress and accessories, and paused at the door. "See you in there. Good luck avoiding the bride."

She joined Mari and Pema outside the cabin.

"Want some lip balm?" Pema offered. "Your lips look chapped."

Mari looked back and forth between Pema and Toni. "Or thoroughly kissed."

Toni's cheeks flamed.

"Wait," Pema said. "I thought you guys were faking it."

"I-I . . ." Toni stammered, not sure how to answer. But these were her friends, and so she blurted, "We aren't really dating, but I want to look better than the bride tonight. Will you help?"

Pema could manage amazing styles with her own long, silvery-white hair—yeti females had a whole other hair thing going on compared to the males. She linked her arm through Toni's. "Absolutely."

Mari took Toni's other arm. "Fuck yeah."

Toni bit her lip, emotion welling at their unquestioning support. "I love you guys so much."

Anticipation fluttered like a million butterflies in her middle when she thought about Denzin and their plans for after the wedding. This would be the best night of her life—so far.

DENZIN TUGGED at his jacket as he stood in front of the floor-to-ceiling windows in the chalet. It might have annoyed some guests to give up their holiday weekend for Julia and Wes, but no one could deny the chalet's views were at their best during clear and cold late November weather. To the north, Denali and Foraker, the tallest peaks in the Alaska Range, caught golden rays of the low angle sun as it began an early descent.

Denzin and Tseten had caved to Julia's request. They'd rearranged the chairs to take advantage of the mountain range panorama. He hadn't only done a favor for the bride, but for all the guests—they would be the ones with the fantastic view during the ceremony. He'd have his back to it as officiant.

He checked his watch and adjusted his cuffs as people filtered in. A drink would have taken the edge off. He could have had a scotch with Tseten but had opted for soda water. Denzin and Toni had hours until they returned to their cabin, but he didn't want to take any chances. Alcohol wouldn't stop them tonight.

As he waited, he found himself imagining what Toni's gown might look like. She'd stored it in an opaque garment bag, and he hadn't asked to see it, opting to be surprised. Given that he was dressed in a black tux, bowtie, and white pocket square—per the bride's request—he couldn't have made changes to coordinated regardless.

A few moments later, his mouth went dry when she stepped into the room. All five-foot eleven of her lithe body rocked a deep red, off-the-shoulder, ankle-length dress. Chatter around the room hushed at her entrance.

Denzin made his way toward her, nearly running over a guest in the process. He couldn't help it. He only had eyes for Antoinette.

A blush the same shade as her gown spread over those lovely cheeks as she watched him approach. If he had his way, he'd be seeing her flush multiple times tonight.

Coming to a stop in front of her, he lifted her hand to his lips. "You're stunning." She was the most beautiful woman in the room.

Her blush deepened. "And you look very handsome, Denzin."

He tugged on the hem of his jacket. "For a yeti."

Face serious, she responded, "No. Human or yeti —you're the best-looking man in this room. Do you have any idea how well you wear a suit? How you exude power and intelligence, command respect? It's extremely attractive."

He blinked, his own face heating. His response was slow to come. "Thank you," he said simply as he tried to recover, her words echoing in his head.

She gave a slight nod, then brought her hand to her hair and turned for him to admire her updo. "Pema outdid herself."

Leaning in, he whispered, "And exposed your elegant neck and chest. During the ceremony, when I look at you, I'll be imagining kissing my way across your decolletage."

He pulled away as her mother approached, leaving Toni to fan herself. The blush now colored her neck and chest, disappearing into her dress and leaving him wondering how far it spread.

"Looking dashing again tonight, Bev," he said while offering his arm. "That's a brilliant color on you."

"Go on with you," she said with a blush of her own as Denzin offered his other arm to Toni and escorted the women to their seats.

The guests might have a view of Denali behind him, but Denzin decided his view was the best. He looked straight at Toni.

Knowing he'd be at her side directly after the ceremony made the entire process of marrying his brother to his ex-girlfriend a lot easier. His hang-up had never been the breakup itself, but the reasons behind it.

Although Toni's earlier praise remained in the forefront of his mind, he'd never received a compliment like that. Not from family or close friends. She'd caught him off guard. It gave him hope. Maybe not all women believed he was as worthless as Julia had made him feel.

Soon, with the power temporarily vested in him by the State of Alaska, Denzin pronounced Wes and Julia husband and wife. Everyone cheered and tossed streamers as the bride and groom paraded down the aisle.

As he slowly trailed in their wake, Toni looped her arm through his, flawlessly joining the procession as if they'd planned it. Denzin held her close.

With their non-alcoholic drinks in hand, he and Toni mingled in the banquet area, where a large, three-tiered cake adorned with frosted pumpkins and vines sat as a centerpiece. Based on Mari's stormy expression, she hadn't missed it. Denzin looked forward to whatever pie she'd bake later this weekend.

After a dinner of turkey curry with cranberry chutney, Bev started in on her line of relationship questions. "Denzin, are you still a climbing guide at

Mountain High?" Translation: "Can you provide for my daughter?"

Denzin opened his mouth to respond when Julia, who'd approached with Wes just as Bev had asked her question, quipped, "He's the head guide."

Toni's glare looked like it could have sliced the bride in half. "Head guide? Is that what you call the regional manager?"

Wes kissed Julia's cheek. "Hon, when we met, and I worked for Mountain High, he held a managerial position."

She shrugged and laughed. "Semantics."

Toni gripped her fork so tightly it looked like she might bend it in half. "As regional manager of Mountain High Guiding Service, Denzin oversees operations of two locations and has started negotiations on a third in Denali. The *Wildwood Weekly* wrote an article about the recent deal he landed with an international cruise ship company for inland tours. It's a boon for Mountain High and Wildwood. It will bring hundreds of tourists into town each summer. Local business owners are thrilled."

Bev looked impressed, and his brother passed a compliment, but Julia appeared nonplussed, not that Denzin cared.

"Right, well great," Julia said. "Wes and I came

over to let you know, Denzin, that the dancing will begin shortly. You can dance with me after Wes and I have the first dance."

Toni placed her balled-up napkin on the table. "Since you're already breaking tradition by not dancing with your father," she said in a tight tone, "why don't Denzin and I join you on the dance floor instead once your song is over? That will encourage others to dance."

Julia looked put out, but Wes quickly agreed and led his bride away as the DJ called for the wedding couple.

Toni turned to Denzin. "Would you like to dance?"

Hold her close to his body and sway to music while showing the entire room how lucky he was? "It would be my pleasure."

She had always been special, but this weekend had opened his eyes. Toni was extraordinary.

CHAPTER EIGHT

Toni was hot, and not in a sexual way. She gripped Denzin's shoulder as he swept her onto the dance floor. "That woman," she grumbled under her breath.

He pulled her closer. "I don't want to talk about Julia. I have an intelligent, beautiful woman in my arms who just defended me and sang my praises. My focus is on you."

Heat prickled across her skin. "You're definitely the better person. And I think I've spent the whole evening blushing in front of you, Denzin."

"I hope that continues."

Her pulse quickened at the meaning behind his words. Warmth from his hand on her lower back radiated through her gown and into her body as they swayed across the floor.

Toni glanced at her mother as they circled around. "I'm sorry that my mother is interrogating you. Again."

"She wants what's best for you."

"And a shirtless salmon fisherman falls into that category?" She shook her head. "I don't understand her contradictions."

"Let's not try to. Her motive is to make sure you're happy and secure."

"What did I say about you being the better person?"

He kissed the top of her head. "I'm glad you're not hooking up with any fishermen this weekend." He drew back a little. "She's dropped that, right?"

Toni laughed. "Yes. For better or worse, her focus is on you now." She nearly added, "For this weekend," but she didn't want to pop their bubble. She was willing to live out this real-life fantasy a few days longer. Then she could ask the tough questions, like what happens next, but only after gaining some firsthand experience with Denzin and those XXL condoms, of course.

She perused the dance floor. Tseten had one arm across Pema's shoulders and the other over Mari's.

The friendly trio's comedic lack of coordination may have been due to them having six legs instead of four —or their patronage of the open bar.

"Are we allowed to leave after this dance?" she half joked.

Denzin's hand dipped lower, fingers skimming the top of her ass, his lips brushing her ear as he said, "We could take a quick break before they cut the cake."

She loved the way he thought, and her blood sped up in anticipation. "You have my attention."

"We could check out the coat closet. See if it's abandoned."

Toni's breath caught, imagining all the things they could do in the back of an overflowing coat closet in the middle of winter in Alaska. "Do we have to finish this dance? This is the longest song ever— not that I mind dancing with you."

His lips quirked in apparent amusement. "What do they say? All good things come to those who wait."

"I think that advice is overrated," she retorted as the song finally ended.

Before Denzin released her, he leaned in and whispered, "I'm going there now. Perhaps collect your purse as if you're heading to the lady's room?

You'll need to reapply that lip gloss when I'm done with you."

A zing of anticipation shot through Toni. Thank god she'd opted for a strapless bra under her gown, or her nips would be on full display for the wedding guests.

While Denzin left the room, she casually returned to their table and picked up her clutch. Her mother and Anne were in deep conversation about hot flashes.

Without a backward glance, which might look suspicious, Toni left the room, walking toward the bathrooms with her head high. Instead of continuing to the chalet's front desk area, she took a hard left and into a room filled with coat racks, but thankfully void of guests.

"Back here," Denzin called softly from behind a full rack.

Toni didn't waste time. She dropped her purse on a small table, wrapped her arms around his neck, and pressed her lips to his. "I've been waiting all evening for this," she admitted between kisses.

When she opened her eyes, she saw red. Literally. "Shit." She wiped at his face. "You have Ripe Cherry Tartlet lip gloss in your fur. And . . ." She squinted. "It might have colored your lips purple."

"Nothing I can't wipe off in the men's room." His lips crushed hers again, his tongue sweeping into her mouth, but his hands held her a few inches away.

She tried to close the distance, but he stopped her. "I don't want to wrinkle your dress."

She looked up at him, a coy smile curling her lips. "Should I take it off?"

He groaned. "I'll remove this gown later when I get to strip you."

"Deal." She grinned, her hands going to the bulge in the front of his pants. "But what about other coat closet fun and games?"

He gently pushed her hand away before finding the slit in her dress. Her thighs quivered under his touch. "I have another idea." He kissed her, his hand moving higher. "If you want to take my cock tonight, we need to get you ready."

She was already aroused, but those words coming from Denzin took her to another level. Her skin tingled, ready for his next move. "What do you have in mind?" she asked with a shaky breath, though she had a pretty good idea as his fingers teased and tickled under her gown.

"I was afraid your stockings would get in the way." He grazed his knuckles across the top of her thigh-highs. "But I don't think that's going to be an issue."

She shook her head.

"I want to see you in those—later," he added.

She wanted to tell him he could fuck her in them, but she could only nod because he'd reached the juncture of her legs, and his big hand palmed her pussy.

"Ms. Antoinette," he said in a low growl, "you're not wearing any underwear. Again."

"Surpr—" The rest of the word turned into a strangled moan as Denzin swirled a finger around her slick clit and slid it inside her. Oh god, it felt good—and big, not dick-sized, but thick for a finger. Her whole body hummed with awareness and pleasure.

He pumped in and out of her, pressing his palm against her clit with each slow, deliberate stroke.

"You're very, very wet."

"I want you," she responded in a pant. Of course she was wet. She ached for him.

"Do you want two fingers?"

"Mmm . . . please." She knew it would be a tight stretch for her, but it would also feel amazing. And as he'd said, it would make her ready for more, for him.

He growled and his chest vibrated under Toni's

palm. He ran a second finger through her folds, coating it in her slickness, then slowly eased both fingers into her.

She exhaled, welcoming the invasion.

His other hand cupped her cheek. "Are you okay? Should I stop?"

"Yes. No. I mean, I'm okay." She nearly growled herself. "Don't you dare stop."

He paused, letting her get accustomed to him while he flicked her clit with his thumb. When she moaned at the sensation, he swallowed it with a kiss.

Toni clung to him. He'd hardly begun to thrust his fingers before the pressure of an intense orgasm quickly rose to the surface. "Fuck, I'm going to—" She went silent, unable to draw in a breath as she squeezed her legs together. She pulsed around Denzin's fingers while waves of pure bliss rippled through her body. She slammed her eyes shut, stars exploding behind closed lids.

When she finally stopped quaking, she released her tight grip on Denzin's jacket. He withdrew his fingers from her and carefully brought his hand out from under her dress.

"That was. Wow. I've never." Toni grasped the back of Denzin's head, went up on her toes, and gave him a hot, wet kiss. "I've never fooled around in public before." She swallowed, her eyes searching his. "And I've never come as hard as I have today. Twice."

A pleased look crossed Denzin's face before he leaned in to kiss her again. A moment later, a loud announcement sounded from the banquet room.

Denzin raised an eyebrow. "Pumpkin cake time?"

More like time to get naked and rip open a condom. But she nodded. "Meet you at the table after freshening up?"

He kissed her cheek, and they left the coat room separately. In the lady's room, Toni latched the door and let out a breath. Denzin might have spared her dress, but she felt—and looked—totally sexed. A flush stained her cheeks and chest. She'd smeared her lip gloss, and no matter how many times she tapped her cheeks, she sported a relaxed look that only came with a toe-curling orgasm.

But no one would know about the delicious tingling between her legs. It reminded her of what she'd share with Denzin later that evening.

NO MATTER how Denzin arranged his tuxedo jacket, his rock-hard erection had to be visible—at least to anyone staring at his crotch. And hopefully, that would only be Toni.

When he made it to the table, she hadn't returned yet. Bev eyed him, though thankfully her gaze appeared steady on his face, and he knew he'd managed to remove all the lip gloss smudges.

"Where's my daughter?"

Denzin motioned toward the door. "I saw her talking to Helen outside the lady's room." He *had* passed Helen on his way back in. It seemed reasonable, or at least possible, that they would have actually run into each other.

Toni slid into her seat a few minutes later when all eyes were turned to the bride, groom, and their big pumpkin cake. Her hand immediately found Denzin's under the table. She'd freshened her makeup and didn't have a hair out of place. Her gown held no more wrinkles than one would expect after wearing it all evening.

But her face looked flushed like she'd been climbing and relaxed like she'd just meditated. Denzin held in a chuckle. "How are you feeling?"

Her lips brushed his ear when she responded, "Like I'm ready for your cock."

He nearly choked. Good thing they were seated and passing around slices of cake. No jacket adjustment could hide his bulge now.

Denzin received two pieces of cake. He gave one to Toni, quietly adding, "You said *cake*, didn't you?"

As she tossed him a withering look, he handed the other piece to Bev. "Pumpkin cake?"

"Such an ingenious idea for a Thanksgiving wedding, don't you think?"

"It seems appropriate for the occasion and the season," Denzin responded diplomatically.

But Toni said, "Come on, Mom, we all wanted pie today. Pumpkin, pecan, sweet potato, even apple."

"Pie isn't traditional for weddings."

"It is for Thanksgiving."

Her mother lowered her eyebrows. "You're eating it."

Around a mouthful of cake, Toni said, "It's from Wildwood Bakery. It's delicious. Of course I'm eating it. But it isn't pie."

"You'd have pie at your wedding?" Bev looked from Toni to Denzin and back as if they'd already discussed marriage and the details of a ceremony. She'd already asked about kids. This seemed a natural progression of her line of questioning.

Denzin stayed mute.

Toni didn't spare him a glance, keeping her eyes on her mother. "I'd think outside the box. That's all I'm saying."

Bev seemed appeased with this but added, "The champagne has flushed your cheeks."

Toni's fork paused midway to her mouth. That blush had everything to do with her coming on Denzin's hand not twenty minutes ago. He and Toni had consumed nothing harder than bubbly water tonight.

A half-filled flute of prosecco sat untouched at her place setting, left over from the toast earlier. "You might be right. You can have this, Mom."

The noise in the room grew louder after the cake. Some people left immediately, while others took advantage of the open bar since they didn't have to drive home. A few showed off a range of mediocre moves on the small dance floor.

Finally, the bride and groom departed under another round of streamers, and Bev declared she would head back to her room for the night. They were free to leave. Denzin's dick pulsed in anticipation of what was to come. "Shall I collect our coats too, Toni?"

She yawned in response. A totally fake yawn.

He tried not to grin.

"Yeah, I'm beat."

Within minutes, they were strolling—okay, more like race walking—hand in hand back to their cabin. A few others were also returning to their own cabins, and some guests who'd driven to the chalet for the wedding were warming up their cars and scraping ice off windshields.

At last he and Toni were alone. The door closed behind them. He threw the deadbolt while Toni adjusted the blinds on the small window.

She turned to him. "Finally."

Denzin helped her out of her coat. "You sound breathless already. Is it from the walk or antic-ipation?"

Toni ran her hands up his chest and pushed his jacket off his shoulders, then held out her hand. It shook. "Not the walk. I'm excited."

He shucked off his jacket then drew a knuckle down the side of her neck, along the collar of her gown, and over the swell of her breasts. When he moved closer to trace the same path with his lips, Toni moaned, looping her arms around his shoulders, holding him to her.

He cupped and kneaded her breast. "I want to

see you, Toni, all of you." Again, his thoughts flashed back to seeing her naked in the shower.

She turned, offering him her back. "You'll have to unzip me."

Fuck, now *his* hands shook. He already knew she wasn't wearing panties, and he'd been imagining her in nothing but heels and her sexy thigh-high stockings since their interlude in the coat closet.

He devoted the same attention to her back as he'd shone to her chest, running his knuckles down her neck and across the defined muscles of her shoulders, following his fingers with slow kisses.

When he reached her zipper, Denzin caught Toni watching him in the mirror. Their eyes locked in the reflection as he slowly unzipped her dress.

When the zipper hit its base, he tore his gaze away from hers to take in the smooth expanse of her back. He lightly ran his fingertips down her spine, over the band of her strapless black bra, and lower to the top of her bare ass.

She shivered in response, bumps rising on her skin. He glanced in the mirror, and the smile that met his in the reflection told him how much she enjoyed his touch.

He eased the dress off her shoulders until it gaped, exposing the front of her lacy bra.

In the mirror, they both watched as he wrapped his large hands around her body, covering her breasts. He lowered his mouth to her neck, placing open-mouthed kisses from behind her ear to the tip of her shoulder while he palmed her.

"Can I remove this?" he asked, indicating her bra.

She nodded, and he fought with the hook until Toni reached back and flicked the clasp open. Then she peeled the fabric away, baring herself to him.

She worried her lip, her eyes now on her own body in the mirror. "They're small. But you probably noticed that already."

He came around and sat on the bed in front of her, blocking her own view and placing himself at eye level with her gorgeous tits. He cupped each one, his thumbs rubbing across her hardened nipples the same dark rose shade as her lips. "Toni, they're perfect." He paused, then growled, "And extremely sexy."

He drew her forward and took one nipple into his mouth, sucking and licking as she gasped. He did the same to the other. "Perfect," he repeated. He could have worshipped her breasts for hours, but he needed to see the rest of her.

He moved behind her again, helping Toni pull

the dress down her hips so she could step out of the garment. Her long legs looked elegant, especially paired with black high-heeled shoes. While he had the urge to toss the dress aside and pull her into his embrace, he instead hung her gown on a hanger, then turned, his hungry gaze devouring her.

"Gods, Toni. You're so beautiful." She stood where he'd left her, legs slightly spread, showcasing black heels and sheer black, thigh-high stockings. And nothing else. Reflected in the mirror, her swollen nipples were a jutting splash of color against her pale skin, and the dark thatch of hair between her legs matched the curls on her head. Her firm ass begged for him to cup it, knead it. And the dimples above her cheeks were as sexy as he'd imagined they would be.

"I want you to take me from behind. I want to watch you in the mirror." Her throat worked as she uttered a word that came out more as a whimper and a plea. "Now."

He stared at her a moment, his cock now harder than ever, before scrambling to remove his own shirt.

Toni's nimble fingers were at his cuff links, his buttons, the fly to his pants. He tossed his clothes over the back of the chair, hanger be damned.

When he was as naked as the day he was born,

he picked Toni up, his hands on those perfect ass cheeks, her legs wrapped around his body. Their mouths crashed together in a tangle of tongues, lips, and teeth.

Balancing her in one arm, he ran a finger through her spread folds. She dripped for him. "You're ready?"

She lowered her hand to the steel rod that was his cock. "So ready. If I wasn't before the coat closet, I am now. One-hundred and twenty percent."

She slid down his body, her feet, in those sexy-ass heels, softly landing on the floor. As he scrambled for a condom, Toni climbed onto the bed on all fours, her gorgeous backside on full display for him.

Over her shoulder, she watched him roll the condom down his length. Her eyelids fluttered when he slid the tip of his cock through her wetness. Then he lined up at her entrance and slowly pushed in.

Fuck. The sensation of sliding into Toni made his entire body buzz with pleasure.

She immediately let out a groan. "God, yes. You feel amazing. More, Zin."

Toni begging for his full length? It nearly undid him then and there.

Their gazes locked in the mirror, chests heaving in unison. Her pussy was tight but slick. He slowly inched forward until his furry hips were flush with her smooth ass, Toni completely impaled on his cock.

He'd never experienced anything this good. He hadn't come yet, and already this was the best sex of his life—because, well, it was with Toni.

TONI'S BODY shook with pleasure. It took a concerted effort to remain on all fours while Denzin filled her from behind. She'd never felt so bold or sexy, demanding a certain position, especially one that left her vulnerable, yet allowed her to watch.

She could have taken him regardless of his preparations in the coat closet, but it had left her stretched and achy with need to be filled by Denzin's extra-large cock. It didn't disappoint. He filled her up so completely.

"You okay?" he asked, one hand gripping her thigh, the other lightly running over her back and ass in an affectionate caress.

She nodded. "So good. I want more."

When he growled, the vibrations passed from his body into hers where they were joined. The sensation hit her like a fucking vibrator. "Oh god," she whimpered.

She tried to rest her weight on one hand and touch herself with the other—her aching nipples, her pulsing clit. But her legs shook so badly that she quickly braced on both hands before she collapsed on her face.

Denzin moved inside her in slow thrusts. As if he knew exactly what she needed, he slid his hands forward, furry arms brushing against her in a delight-fully soft rub along sensitive skin. He gently tugged on her nipples, rolling them between his fingers and sending sparks through her body. Her eyes fluttered shut and she focused on the sensation of him moving inside her, caressing her body.

His rhythm increased, pulling out and gliding back in with a grind of his hips as his hand traveled lower. His steel-blue gaze sometimes on her body, other times catching hers in the mirror—when she could keep her eyes open.

Soon his fingers found her clit, and she cried out, waves of pleasure rippling through her.

In response, Denzin moved faster. And she met him, thrusting back into his solid furry body as he pushed into her. The force made her breasts bounce with the movement. Each deep thrust took her body to a higher point, winding her tighter.

Through a haze of bliss, her dark eyes caught his

piercing blue gaze, now brightened by lust and pleasure.

"I'm so close," she moaned.

He growled in return and pounded her harder, faster. One finger worked her swollen clit, the other hand kneading her breast. She began to spasm around him, clutching at his cock as if she could possibly pull more from him.

As she peaked, Denzin roared behind her. Her own final cry sucked the air from her lungs. His cock pulsed inside her body as he also found his release with one last shuttering thrust.

They stayed locked together, their chests both heaving with the effort. A bead of sweat rolled between Toni's breasts.

"Toni." Denzin's voice came out hoarse, strained, like he'd also just run a marathon. His hands ran lightly over her back and down her legs, over the stockings that had rolled down one leg and were likely full of runs.

She didn't care.

Denzin tried speaking again. "That was . . . I've never . . ."

She nodded at him in the mirror before lowering to her elbows, not wanting to lose sight of him, but giving in to her body's total exhaustion. "Me neither,

Denzin. That was amazing." Turned out, there was a better feeling than successfully climbing a difficult route—sex with Denzin.

He pulled out from her, and she immediately missed the full feeling of him inside her. She grew cold without his warm, furry body against hers.

While he disposed of the condom, she let herself crumple into a heap, rolling to her side.

When Denzin returned, his fingers blazed a slow, hot trail from her hip to her ankle, then slipped off her shoe. He rolled a stocking down her leg with a tender sweep of his giant hand, repeating his actions on her other leg.

His eyes dipped to her swollen sex, and his lids lowered. "You have no idea how fucking hot you look right now."

Her core pulsed at the compliment, but she was too exhausted for round two. He scooped her up, and she wound herself around him as he pulled back the covers. They slid under the sheets together.

As he turned out the light, she purred, "Denzin."

She wanted to tell him how she felt. Happier than she ever had been. More sated. Cared for. Loved. Her heart raced at the L-word. She pushed that away. They were friends—now with benefits—

nothing more. Instead, she focused on how good it felt to be in his arms.

When she said nothing further, he pulled her closer, and tangled her legs with his, fur tickling and caressing as it brushed against her skin.

He pressed a kiss to her forehead. "Sweet dreams, Toni."

Being in Denzin's arms guaranteed sweet dreams.

CHAPTER NINE

The morning after the wedding, Toni knew exactly where she was when she woke up— on top of Denzin again. Even after their sexcapades, it still thrilled her.

Only this time, they were both naked, and her girly bits suffered from a hangover.

Denzin's gentle fingers brushed her hair away from her face as her eyelashes fluttered open. "Good morning, beautiful."

Toni wanted to wake up every day to his deep, rumbling voice. She attempted to return the greeting, but only managed a, "Mmm."

"How are you feeling?" He feathered a hand over her backside, and her skin came alive in response.

"Like I need a bottle of mouthwash."

He chuckled. "We didn't even floss last night."

She smiled, but her fingers worried the fur on his chest. She knew what he was really asking about. Her body, her feelings. Her heart began to pound in both excitement and nervousness, thrilled at what they'd finally done, that she'd woken in his arms again. But what happened next?

She focused on the physical, wriggling her hips and shifting her legs. "I'm a little sore, but in a good way."

"There's a good sore?"

"Yeah, of course. Sore muscles after a hard climb or a long hike are satisfying. You worked hard and pushed your body to accomplish something remarkable."

The corners of his mouth turned up. "We certainly accomplished something remarkable last night."

She let out a soft laugh. "I agree, though I'm feeling less bold this morning."

He stilled under her. "Do you regret—?"

Toni lifted her head. "No, no. Not at all. I'm just . . ." She buried her face in the crook of his arm. "Feeling shy. I've never . . . been so . . . so insistent. I can't even blame alcohol." What really bothered her were the thoughts she kept trying to push away. How would she look him in the eye at work, especially now that he'd fucked her into next week—at her own demand?

A growl worked its way out of Denzin's chest. He shifted to lie next to Toni and looked down at her as he ran a reassuring hand along her side.

She couldn't help but toss an arm over her eyes though, as a wave of self-consciousness washed over her.

"We haven't talked about our past partners much. You know about Julia, clearly. And yeti can't exactly hook up at the bar with someone new each weekend. But I can honestly say that what we shared last night was the hottest sex I've ever had."

She moved her arm to peek at him, her body flushing with heat.

"The way you stated what you wanted—so hot. A turn-on." He kissed her cheek, his voice lowering. "And I was more than happy to accommodate your wishes. I wanted it too. I wanted you."

He feathered his hand under Toni's breast. Her nipple puckered and breath hitched. "If we had more time—and you weren't sore—I'd worship you this morning, Toni, slowly loving every inch of your body."

This time, her breath hitched for an entirely different reason. That sounded a lot like making love, not casual sex between two friends who'd embarked on a silly pact to ensure they weren't alone for a wedding. That would be harder to walk away from. Returning to work on Monday to face Denzin and her coworkers would be hard enough already. And she didn't want to think about the handful of other locals at the wedding who now thought she and Denzin were involved.

If this were a Cinderella story, the clock would be nearing midnight, and far too late for sharing feelings with the prince. Toni didn't intend to lose a heel on her way out the door. She wore running shoes, ready to make a quick escape.

"What time is it?" she asked, painfully aware that her question was not a suitable response to his declaration.

He reached for his phone on the nightstand, seemingly taking it in stride. "Quarter past nine," he said, then brushed a thumb along her cheek. "Toni, we don't have to do anything you don't want to do."

Was she that transparent? Apparently. "The brunch is at ten thirty, and we have to pack and be out of our cabin beforehand." She quickly added, "We're a little pressed for time, that's all."

They totally had time to linger in bed. Why had she been so bold yesterday, only to become nervous and timid today?

Because they were now in their final act. The wedding was over, and Wes and Julia would depart after brunch. Toni and Denzin would soon vacate the magic of the secluded cabin. For the duration of the weekend, Toni had to make sure her mother didn't have a reason to question Toni's relationship with Denzin. But that seemed guaranteed at this point.

Denzin laid a hand on Toni's hip, his blue eyes studying her face as if trying to know and understand all the thoughts running through her complicated head. She couldn't comprehend most of them. No way he could.

Finally, he asked, "Do you want the first shower while I see if the instant coffee is any good? Maintenance fixed the rod."

She sat up, grateful that he hadn't pressed for sex, hadn't questioned her. "I *am* looking forward to a shower," she admitted.

Denzin paused, giving her one last look. "Are we okay?"

Toni tried her hardest to give him a genuine smile. "Of course we are," she lied. Then she fled to the bathroom and hid from the one person who meant more to her than anyone else.

DENZIN STARTED the electric kettle as the shower pounded on the other side of the wall. Toni needed space, and he didn't want to pressure her. He wouldn't interrupt her shower this time, and his bathroom time would be equally solitary. He tried not to let it discourage him.

Denzin didn't want Toni to regret what they'd done. After waking up yesterday morning with her in his arms, the sexual tension between them had been unlike anything he'd experienced.

But sex changed things between people, and their situation was difficult, especially for Toni. He'd hired her, filled the role of "boss" when they were in the office. No getting around that. And he would provide a professional atmosphere when they returned to work on Monday.

However, outside of work, they needed to determine their next step. They seemed so natural together. Why not explore an actual relationship beyond the weekend? That was what he wanted. Didn't she want the same? Maybe she didn't like him the way he liked her. Julia's rejection loomed large. Toni could like Denzin but not be on board with the limitations of dating a yeti.

Denzin poured boiling water into a second cup of instant coffee once the shower turned off. Better to let the coffee cool out here than to bring a hot cup to Toni and invade her space.

Instead, Denzin turned to his tux, hastily discarded on a chair last night. By the time Toni came out of the bathroom—fully dressed—he'd packed all his things except for the clothes he'd wear to the brunch. He showered quickly, and they soon closed the door on the Aurora cabin.

Short, awkward, trivial conversation filled the time on their walk to the chalet. Brunch turned out to be informal. Steaming chafing dishes lined a wall, and several dispersed groups sat at the round tables. He and Toni joined her mother.

"Can you believe it?" Bev said over a melon ball. "Wes and Julia already left."

Toni gave Denzin a side-eye. "Did you know they intended to do that?"

Denzin stifled a sigh and tried to hide the disappointment that tied knots in his stomach as he drew his phone from his pocket. He'd fucking married them yesterday, and they hadn't said good-bye. "Looks like I missed a text. Yes, they've left to catch an early flight." Or so he gathered from Julia's promise to send a postcard from France. He didn't show the message to Toni. Yesterday, he might have shared it, confided in her. But given the distance Toni had wedged between them, he didn't want to expose his vulnerabilities in front of her right now.

Her lips flattened anyway, as if she guessed that Wes and Julia basically ghosted him.

"Well, if they're not here for us to send them off and wish them well, then I'm skipping the orange juice in my mimosa and going to see if there's left-over wedding cake in the back." Bev rose. "I'll bring you a piece, Antoinette. If you put it under your pillow, you'll dream of Denzin, I'm sure."

Mari, Pema, and Tseten walked up at that moment.

"Dream of Denzin?" Mari asked.

Bev drained her champagne flute before answering, "If you place wedding cake under your pillow, you'll dream about the person you'll marry."

Real smooth, Bev. Denzin stole a glance at Toni. She'd turned a deep shade of cranberry as everyone looked at them with knowing smiles. But they didn't actually know anything.

Toni practically growled. "If you bring me a slice of cake, Mom, I'm going to eat it."

Mari moved to Bev's side. "I'm still upset that we didn't get pie on Thanksgiving, but I'll go with you and wrap a piece for Dorje."

"I'll sleep on cake, Bev," Tseten volunteered. "I dream about Rosa most nights, so it may mean nothing if she appears in my dreams. Of course, if I don't dream about her—or anyone . . ." A deep frown creased his face. "I'll be heartbroken."

"If that happens, eat the squished cake when you get up. And you'll always have me, cuz." Pema gave him a cheesy grin. "Bring me a slice. To eat. Wedding cake for breakfast sounds like a good way to start the day. I'm not marrying anyone, so why smoosh perfectly good cake under my pillow?"

Mari's mother joined the table a moment later, setting her plate next to Toni.

"The others are raiding the kitchen for wedding cake," Pema informed her. "The bride left it behind."

Anne grinned and draped a napkin in her lap. "The perfect complement to reindeer sausage and gravy."

"There's really nothing that doesn't go with

cake," Pema added before amending, "When the cake is good."

The two chatted as Denzin and Toni sat in what seemed like noticeable silence. He eventually turned to her. "More coffee?"

A tight, appreciative smile pulled across her face, and she handed him her mug. But her eyes didn't quite meet his.

When he returned with a carafe for the table, the trio emerged from the kitchen with a whole tier of cake, zip-top bags, and two bottles of sparkling wine.

Bev sipped from her flute and dispersed small pieces of cake in zip-top bags to whoever would take one. She foisted a bag at Toni despite her objections. "Put this under your pillow tonight or in the freezer. Don't let it go bad."

Denzin wanted to slide his arm around Toni, letting her know he supported her. But he got the impression that he'd only make her feel worse if he showed any physical affection right now. He draped his arm on her chair for show but didn't touch her. They were supposedly faking it for Bev's benefit, after all.

By the time the group reduced the cake to crumbs and drained the bottles, their collective volume had risen several decibels, fueled by sugar and alcohol. Only he and Toni hadn't partaken in the juiceless mimosas.

Bev drained her glass and turned to him. "I suppose you're taking us to Toni's house since you and she arrived together." Her eyes darted between the two of them. "Have you talked about moving in together? It would make financial sense."

Again, all eyes at the table focused on them.

Denzin opened his mouth to say, "We're on no particular timeline."

But Toni shot her mother a lethal look. "Stop interfering, Mom."

She raised a hand in innocence. "What? Seems like a natural question to ask." She rested an elbow on the table and turned to Denzin. "Are you still living in your family's home, off Birch Drive?"

When he confirmed as much, she added. "I'd love to see your place again. Toni and I could bring a crock pot of soup up tomorrow."

As Toni protested, Denzin agreed to it. He didn't have any ready excuses for not having guests over, plus Rab and Helen would be staying with him until they flew back to Toklat Lodge. "Everyone is welcome. Bring a dish to share."

Tseten raised his glass. "Potluck at Denzin's house."

Denzin didn't know what Toni wanted or needed. Another group meal might be a bad idea, but he was committed to it now. Hopefully, before tomorrow night, he and Toni could clear the air and enjoy the evening.

CHAPTER TEN

Toni's phone buzzed with a text from Denzin. Another request to talk before the potluck.

Her face heated remembering her dream last night. She'd been tempted to eat the bag of cake her mother had foisted on her at bedtime, but eating in bed was just gross. She'd shoved it under her damn pillow. She hadn't slept well, but of course she'd dreamed of Denzin. A given, after all they'd shared together. But the PG content of the dream bothered her the most. It didn't involve XXL condoms or thick yeti fingers, but a field of wild iris, a sweet kiss in the ice cave—not as teenagers, as adults. So confusing.

Her mother's loud voice yanked her focus from her phone and daydreams. "You're not listening to me," she complained as she stirred the crock pot.

"Does Denzin like spicy food? Should I add green chile to the soup or not?"

Toni's phone buzzed again before she could answer. This time it was Mari asking how things were with Denzin.

A muscle pulsed in Toni's jaw. She took a deep breath to calm her nerves. She owed Denzin a response and explanation but wasn't certain what to say to him. Mari was concerned about her. And her mother showed consideration for Denzin's preferences. A good thing, not something meant to torment Toni.

"I'm not sure, Mom. Why don't you bring the chile? You can always add it at his house."

"Good thinking." She opened the cupboard for a container. "When your cornbread is cool, we'll be ready to go. I just need to change."

Toni nodded weakly. "It's already cool enough for a lid."

"Great, I'll go get ready." Her mother paused and cupped Toni's cheek. "Your headache feeling better today? You still look pale."

Claiming a headache excused her current mood. "It's better than it was," she lied. Headache or not, Toni felt rotten.

While her mother changed, Toni turned back to

her phone, first looking at the string of messages she hadn't replied to. She hadn't talked to Denzin since he'd driven them home yesterday after brunch. He'd texted several times, not enough to be annoying. The perfect amount. Because he was perfect, damn it.

She hadn't known how to reply. They'd rushed into this outrageous dating plan without giving it much thought. And then she'd given in to the intense chemistry between them, pushing all doubts aside while she went with her feelings, her gut. Or perhaps more accurately, her hormones.

But the doubts were back, and they kept multiplying like gremlins in water.

Toni also avoided answering Mari's text. She hadn't decided if she'd confess it all to her friend— that she'd had sex with Denzin, and her emotions now spanned the spectrum from elated to terrified.

She felt raw, vulnerable, and unsteady, as if her foundation was shifting beneath her, threatening to topple the new life she'd built in Alaska. Toni hated it.

Instead of responding to the messages, she pulled open a map. One other slight hiccup—Toni had only been to Denzin's once since she'd moved back. The subdivision below his family's house had grown. New, wider roads had replaced narrow, winding tracks. She didn't know how to get to her "boyfriend's" home.

As Toni pulled up a map on her phone and tried to memorize where to turn onto his road, her mother rounded the corner with the slow cooker. They loaded the car and headed to the party Denzin had to throw because of Toni and her meddlesome mother.

Toni only took one wrong turn on the way to his house. If her mother noticed, she didn't mention it, instead reminiscing about old neighbors who'd lived in Wildwood before Toni was born.

Even with the slight detour, they were the first to arrive. Thankfully Helen and Rabten were staying with him and would provide a needed buffer—Toni and her mother wouldn't be alone with Denzin.

Toni carried the soup and followed her mother along a shoveled path to the front door. Denzin's two-story log home sat on a small knob among thinned birch trees, allowing for a panoramic view of the surrounding area.

"Oh," her mother gasped. "Look." She pointed to ice lanterns, glowing with the dancing light of tea candles. "They're so lovely," she gushed.

As she paused to admire the flickering glow, she turned to Toni and said, "I always wondered if you and Denzin would end up together. I know you had a crush on him when you were in high school. Those other boys couldn't turn your head. You only had eyes for him. He's a very special person. I'm not only elated that you're no longer single, but also because you're with him."

The wild tempo of Toni's heart only became more erratic when Denzin cleared his throat. He stood in the front door. But with the wedding over, Toni couldn't help but see her boss standing there, not her supposed boyfriend. And he'd likely heard every word her mother had said. She suddenly felt like that high school girl again, embarrassment flushing her cheeks.

If Denzin heard, he didn't let on. "It's not fully dark, but I lit the candles anyway."

At some point this winter, Denzin had made the ice lanterns. Images of him around his house, busy with crafty domestic tasks, warmed her heart and filled her head, no matter how hard she tried to push them out.

Denzin stepped forward. "Thanks for coming. Can I help you with that?"

"We invited ourselves," Toni reminded him, as he shouldered a bag from her mother and moved to take the slow cooker.

He leaned forward as if to kiss Toni's cheek, and her stomach clenched. She wanted that kiss, but it also terrified her. Her panic must have been visible. Denzin drew back, stormy blue eyes fleetingly meeting hers before he turned away to trail her mother inside. "Let's get this pot plugged back in. Helen and Rab are in the kitchen, baking bread. The others should arrive soon."

Denzin followed Toni's cues and didn't force conversation. Soon the house filled, allowing Toni to keep her distance from Denzin without being obvious. Her mother seemed none the wiser. Mari brought four pies. Over the course of the evening, Toni helped herself to a slice of each. They were delicious and—for the moment—made her feel better.

Toni was loading her plate into the dishwasher when her mother cornered her, a huge smile on her face.

"There you two are," she said.

Toni turned and realized that Denzin had entered the kitchen from the other direction.

Her mother held up her phone. "I changed our tickets for Christmas," she declared. "I did it all on the app. Tseten connected me with your Wi-Fi, Denzin." She looked so proud of herself.

"What do you mean 'our tickets,' Mom? I'm coming to see you over Christmas. You bought me a ticket. I'll return before New Year's so I can go out to the Toklat Lodge for Rab's party like last year. There's only one ticket. My ticket."

"But then Denzin would have been alone for Christmas. I canceled your ticket and booked my own to be here in Wildwood. Now you, me, and Denzin can all spend Christmas together."

Toni glanced at Denzin, then quickly scanned the immediate crowd. They were far from alone, because she'd made sure that no one could isolate her and demand to know her feelings. How could she share what she couldn't understand?

It might have been her imagination, but everyone seemed to turn and listen to their conversation. To see how she'd deal with the Thanksgiving charade expanding to another holiday.

Suddenly, four pieces of pie seemed like a bad idea as they roiled in her stomach. Well, fuck. She hadn't seen this coming.

DENZIN MOVED to put an arm around Toni, but stopped before making contact. Hopefully Bev wouldn't realize he wasn't actually touching his "girlfriend."

"How thoughtful of you, Bev. But I have Christmas plans already." He needed to shut this down—or at least remove himself from their plans.

Bev and Toni simultaneously responded with, "You do?"

Toni turned slightly as if noticing the arm that wasn't quite around her. He pulled it behind his back and clasped his hands together. Tightly.

"As Toni mentioned at the wedding, we're in early negotiations to open an office in Denali. I'll be up there for work over solstice and then will head to Toklat early."

At least, now he would be. Toni had access to his work calendar since she scheduled many of the events at the Mountain High office. He made a mental note to update his agenda before she arrived at work on Monday.

Helen slid her arm around Rab and added, "With two yeti on the task, the lodge will have the biggest decorated tree for hundreds of miles."

This whole situation was getting out of hand. They'd lied and were now telling more lies to keep one person from knowing they weren't in an actual relationship. Their friends were going along with the lies as if he and Toni's relationship was valid and expected. And it *had* felt real.

Toni hadn't been the only one with a crush. Now that he'd finally had her in his arms, he ached to hold her again. To stop pretending and acknowledge their feelings and find a way to be together.

To Bev, he said, "I'm sure you and Toni will have a lovely holiday whether you spend it here or in Seattle."

Bev put a hand on her hip, her mouth down-turned in obvious disappointment. Because he'd foiled her clever plan, or because they wouldn't all be together in that family unit that she so clearly wanted for Toni? He wasn't sure. "Well. I—" she began.

Toni held up a placating hand. "Let's talk about it tomorrow morning before your flight, Mom. We'll figure it out."

Denzin rubbed his hands together, ready to change the subject and remove himself from this discussion. "Several people have asked that I get the fire pit going. Excuse me, ladies, while I light up the night."

No one had asked for a fire. The idea had tumbled out of his mouth. He needed an excuse for fresh air and to be by himself.

He stepped away and immediately jogged down the stairs and out to the fire pit, only bothering with a jacket because sparks and fur didn't mix. Once outside, he took several deep breaths, then loaded his arms with so much firewood his muscles strained to carry it all—a necessary physical distraction. He hauled enough wood to keep a fire going until spring.

A couple hours later, as folks packed up and his nerves had settled some, Denzin decided he needed to step up. One of them had to stop running. Things would only get worse if they didn't talk about what had happened between them, how they were feeling. He was not as open with his emotions as Tseten, but it wouldn't do them any good to bottle things up.

When Toni went inside, he waited a beat before following and catching up with her. "Toni," he called to her back. "Can I talk to you for a minute?"

Even with her coat on, he could see her shoulders rise and tense. Not surprising. At this point, talking wouldn't be comfortable for either of them, but it still needed to happen.

She turned and nodded, looking resigned, like her plan to dodge him all night had just failed.

Denzin led her into a side room and turned on a lamp.

"Your old bedroom," she observed, her eyes darting around. "In high school."

He nodded. "We were more cramped for space then." The house had been full to overflowing with his grandparents, mom, birth father, and Wes. "I moved upstairs a long time ago."

He owned the rambling house now and lived in it alone. His mother had willed it to him, and the yeti-friendly law firm, Creer and Associates, had made sure the title bore his name. Those details could be tricky for yeti.

"Toni, I'm sorry if our arrangement for the wedding made you uncomfortable. I didn't expect it to go as far as it did." Images of her naked body, ass turned up to him, filled his mind. He scrubbed a hand across his face, struggling to focus. "But I don't have any regrets. I like you, Toni. I enjoyed having you by my side this week, in my arms, in my bed."

He heard her intake of breath, but when she didn't reply, he pushed on. "I don't want this to be fake. We didn't have to pretend anything this weekend. I know that dating a yeti wouldn't be easy, but we have chemistry. My feelings for you are real. I'd like to explore this and see where it goes."

Toni held her arms across her body like a shield, her face pulled tight with an emotion he couldn't read. It pained him to see her this way. "Denzin, I . . ."

The outside door whooshed open and closed. Rab's deep voice called, "Zin?"

Denzin wanted to pull Toni into a hug. Hold her. Reassure her. Instead he quickly said, "Please think about it. You know how I feel, where I stand. I won't push the matter if you're not interested. And we're both adults and professionals. We'll make this work—either way—when we're back in the office."

Heart in his throat, he tore his gaze from Toni after she nodded, and he left the room. She clearly didn't have a quick answer for him, and he wanted to give her time and space to consider his proposition. He didn't want to think of this as a game, but the ball was in her court now.

CHAPTER ELEVEN

M onday morning, Toni rolled up to the Wild Brew coffee hut window. "A sixteen-ounce sludge, please."

The barista arched an eyebrow. "That's a departure from your usual soy latte. Fighting a Thanksgiving weekend family hangover?"

"Something like that." Toni tried to laugh it off, but her face fell the moment she sped off with her beverage. She didn't normally opt for a shot of espresso in her coffee. Today, she needed it. Sleep was a distant memory. She hadn't caught a solid wink since the wedding when she and Denzin had fallen into a sated, post-orgasmic slumber while wrapped around each other's bodies.

On Saturday, he'd confessed to liking her,

wanting more. She should feel elated. Instead, his confession had sent her spiraling. It would have been easier to leave a weekend fling behind if neither felt strong emotions or if she'd been the only one feeling them. She could have ignored her own feelings if it meant protecting her career and reputation—she'd already been doing that for nearly a year.

Toni halted her mental free fall by focusing on two things Denzin had said—they were adults and professionals. With that in mind, she threw her shoulders back, lifted her chin, and marched into the Mountain High Guiding Service office.

She wasn't sure how to proceed with Denzin, but she knew he wouldn't discuss their relationship at work. Today she'd swapped her proverbial running shoes for skates. The ice might be thin, but she was determined to glide. Still, she'd purposefully skipped breakfast knowing that her stomach would flip the moment she set eyes on Denzin.

She started the computer at the front desk. While it booted, she took a long pull from her drink, not that it would calm her nerves. She should absolutely not check Denzin's schedule the second the computer came to life. But did he really have a trip planned to Denali before Christmas? If he didn't, she'd know for sure that he'd dodged her mother's scheming, and if he did . . . well, it would be news to her, but not unexpected. Mountain High was pursuing a business opportunity in Denali and maybe the visit had been in the works.

Unable to stop herself, she clicked on the shared calendar. Denzin *did* have a trip to Denali scheduled on the nineteenth of December. He'd be meeting with the owner of Denali Powder. Huh.

The small outfitter had been around for years, and the owners were contemplating retirement and the sale of their business. Denzin also had a call with them today.

She rolled her eyes at her overreach and promptly closed the calendar. That had not been a professional move on her part. She hated that she'd checked. Maybe she had more in common with her mother, and the woman's intrusive nature, than she realized.

Usually Toni said good morning to Denzin, and they chatted briefly about the day while she watered the plants in his office. The job was hers because she'd given him the plants—his backroom office had needed the greenery, the cheer—but he'd warned her they'd have brief lives under his care.

Since it would be unusual for her to not say good morning, she grabbed the watering can and marched upstairs to his office. Ignoring the ball of tension in her gut, she gave his door a rap and identified herself.

"Come in." His voice was deep, authoritative. Every bit a leader. A boss.

It gave her a thrill. She loved it—too much. Her chest swelled with emotion as she entered the code— a damn betrayal of her own body. Denzin's commanding nature was part of what made him attractive. He'd been a natural leader, even when they were young.

With a calming hand to her belly, she entered. Denzin's office suited him. Like most mornings, he'd raised his desk to standing level. He faced the tinted windows where a thin band of light blue lined the horizon, a promise of sunrise still hours away. In his right hand, he squeezed and released a red stress ball.

She pushed the guilt aside. He always had the stress ball in hand. It didn't mean anything.

"Good morning," she managed, trying her best to ignore his scent. Juniper and sandalwood would forever make her heart thump uncontrollably against her ribs. The water in the can rippled as her hands shook.

He turned then, his chest rising with a deep breath. "Good morning," he returned. "Do we have school groups scheduled today?"

Her shoulders relaxed a fraction. She'd known he wouldn't ask about the weekend. Not here, not now. But she'd still had doubts, like always. Toni crossed the room to a bushy spider plant. "Yes," she answered, as she poured a stream of water into the pot like it was any other Monday. "A group this morning, another this afternoon, and more tomorrow and Wednesday."

"The new guy—Jeremy—will be here to help you?"

She nodded, moving to a small lily that had wilted, missing the water she normally gave it at the end of the week. "Since he didn't show up last week, I messaged him to confirm he's coming in. He'll help with the morning group, and I'll train him on the booking system. Eddie will be here for our staff meeting and to help with the second group."

He hummed in acknowledgment. "I have a ten-thirty call with Nordic Cruises."

Finally, she could give him a genuine smile. "Another cruise line? Zin, that's fantastic. I assume they're also looking for glacier-type tours?" She moved around to the other plants. They'd seemed to multiply over the past ten months.

"Yes, although they mostly operate north of here, out of Denali. These are long game talks, relationship building. I also have a one thirty with Denali Powder."

"Are the owners of Mountain High any closer to talking them into selling?"

Denzin leaned on his desk. "Another long game," he said, eyes on her perhaps a fraction too long before turning to his computer screen.

Did he think of *her* as a long game?

The plants were watered, she and Denzin had discussed the day's activities, and the new guy arrived in fifteen minutes. Toni paused, jaw clenching, ready to make her exit. "Uh, well, back to it," she said before leaving Denzin to his work while she returned downstairs.

Okay. Alright. This could work. If every day was like this morning, perhaps pretending to date at the wedding and begging her boss to pound his XXL . . . Toni sucked in a breath, her cheeks going hot. What was she thinking? She would not finish that thought at work.

She fanned her face and pretended her mind hadn't gone there. Perhaps attending the wedding together wouldn't affect her job. And maybe no one in town, outside of their friends, would know they'd gone to the wedding together. This might just fade without attention. She still didn't know what to do about Denzin's feelings for her, but at least she knew what was possible between them at work.

Jeremy arrived with a scowl on his face, though he brightened when the school group trooped in. The wilderness safety talk and demo of the bouldering wall went well enough.

The scowl returned when Toni ran through the booking system with him. Again. He'd deleted the example database. Twice. She patiently restored it for him and encouraged him to try once more while she busied herself across the room, but his mood only soured.

As he shoved into his jacket before leaving, he paused, a hint of a sneer pulling at his upper lip. "I hear you're dating the boss. A lot of people at the brewery were talking about it."

Toni blinked, the weight of his words crashing into her like a tsunami. She tried to calm down and think rationally. Okay, so there was some gossip after all. It didn't necessarily mean people would judge her. Her reply was curt. "My personal life is none of your business."

He flipped his collar. "Isn't it? I get this situation now. You got a holiday bonus—I saw it, don't deny it. I didn't. You aren't even a direct employee. Eddie reprimanded me for arriving a few minutes behind schedule. But no one batted an eye when you came in over an *hour* late a few weeks ago."

Heat burned her cheeks as she sputtered, "I helped my neighbor out of the ditch." As soon as the words were out she inwardly groaned. She didn't need to defend herself against his claims. Did she?

"No one even asked for my excuse before handing out an immediate admonishment." He paused, and smirked. "Now I know why I'm getting harassed, and you're getting extra checks."

Blood drained from Toni's face. If she hadn't just slept with the boss, she'd be pissed. But today, guilt crept in. Was this guy right? No, absolutely not. Maybe?

Bonuses were discretionary, handed out by Denzin. There were many reasons that Jeremy wouldn't have received one. But should Toni have received a bonus since she wasn't a direct employee? She tried not to show how Jeremy's words twisted her inside.

"We both know that I don't need you to babysit me. I can do all this on my own." His eyes flit toward the staircase that led to Denzin's office, to a boss he'd never met. "But he lets you do whatever you want, doesn't he? Even at the detriment to his business and his staff. He doesn't need two of us billing hours for the same shift, and you're not giving me the chance I deserve to do this on my own." He paused a beat then scoffed, "Who do I have to sleep with to get ahead?"

Toni's hands trembled with embarrassment and anger. She balled them into fists. "You are totally out of line."

He might be out of line, but he could be right. Had Denzin given her special treatment? Since all their friends had recognized the heat in their New Year's Eve kiss, she couldn't deny that the attraction between herself and Denzin had started long before the wedding weekend. Their ruse had simply brought it out into the open. She suddenly felt raw, exposed.

He raised his hands in mock surrender. "I'm just connecting the dots and can't help but wonder how you got a grant for the climbing wall when others have tried and failed."

There were many reasons why Toni had succeeded in receiving the grant, but nausea still threatened, her stomach churning. "I worked hard to receive funding for the climbing wall." Her voice had an annoying shake to it, and her mouth felt like a dried-out jar of school paste, but she pushed on. "Any suggestion to the contrary is untrue and insulting, and I do not have to defend myself. You need to leave, Jeremy."

His face transformed into an ugly, satisfied leer when the door opened behind him, and a customer came in.

Jeremy turned and left as the customer, oblivious to the tension, bustled up to the counter. A Rudolph pin on her jacket blinked a merry red light as she requested holiday gift cards.

Toni stared at the woman for a beat. What if she also knew that Toni had slept with her boss? Would the woman judge her? Toni's hands went clammy. But nothing out of the ordinary passed between them, and Eddie arrived for the staff meeting during the transaction. With a cheery wave, he headed up to Denzin's office. Meanwhile, Toni's whole body shook from the flood of adrenaline released during her confrontation with Jeremy,

As soon as the woman left with her purchase, Toni flipped the Be Right Back sign and locked the front door so they wouldn't be disturbed during their staff meeting. She grabbed a notebook and dashed up the stairs, her heart still beating overtime.

Coming to a stop outside Denzin's office door, Toni bent at the waist, rested her hands on her knees, and took a deep breath—calming herself as if she'd just sprinted up a mountain. When she stood, she tried to school her features before going in, but she clearly hadn't done a good enough job based on the look Denzin gave her when she entered.

"Something wrong?" he asked.

She didn't want to say anything in front of Eddie. What if Eddie agreed with Jeremy? What if they all thought that Denzin showed her favoritism? She wasn't even sure what to say to Denzin, how to explain what had happened.

She forced a smile and shook her head as she slid into a chair next to Eddie and opened her notebook. "I just sold two gift cards." She'd tried for an upbeat tone, but it fell flat.

Eddie rested his ankle on his knee. He didn't even have a notebook. More comfortable as a guide, management responsibilities were new to him. He cracked a sly smile. "Pema told me you two went to the wedding together. So, what's happening here? Are you guys really dating?"

And that was the straw that broke the camel's back.

Toni leapt to her feet at the same time Denzin unleashed a feral snarl.

"I'm not feeling well," she mumbled. Which was true. She'd never felt sicker. Eddie's question might have been innocent enough, but on the heels of Jeremy's accusation, it triggered Toni's instinct to run, flee, and find a safe place. Her insecurities suddenly made her feel like everyone in Wildwood would question her motivations and credibility. She felt like a fraud.

A crash and deep harsh words from Denzin sounded behind her, but Toni barreled down the stairs. Her nightmare was coming true—everything she'd worked for, owning her own business and setting up a new, adult life in Alaska, felt like it was crashing down around her.

———

DENZIN PACED HIS OFFICE. Every bone in his body wanted to slam Eddie against the wall for making a comment that had triggered Toni, but Eddie wasn't to blame. Denzin was angry with himself.

No one had forced him to call Toni his girlfriend and bring her to the wedding. He'd known better. He was the boss, tasked with making the best decisions for everyone under his management. But he'd been selfish. Denzin had gone along with the plan under the pretext of helping Toni, but he'd been jealous.

He hadn't wanted Toni dating some shirtless fisherman—or anyone else for that matter. He'd wanted her for himself.

Eddie lifted his arms in surrender. "What did I say? You and Toni attended the wedding, right? We all figured you two would get together at some point. There's nothing wrong with that."

"Yes and no," Denzin ground out. "Because I signed the contract for her services, I'm technically her boss. Many workplaces don't allow relationships between management and those who report to them, for good reason." He scrubbed a hand over his chin. "Regardless of where Toni and I stand now, we acted all weekend as if we were a couple. That puts her in a vulnerable position."

Understanding dawned on Eddie's face. "Yeah, but none of us would accuse Toni of sleeping with the boss for favoritism or whatever. And we all know you would never take advantage of her."

"It doesn't matter what we think. It's the public perception and how she feels about it, that matters." He grabbed his stress ball and squeezed. "Fuck," he hissed. "I should never have agreed to that fake dating scheme."

He turned as his pacing reached a wall. "Don't you have a school group to prepare for?" he growled, wincing at his harsh tone, one he couldn't control.

Eddie raised an eyebrow, but quickly made his exit. The door clicked shut a moment later plunging Denzin into a ringing silence.

He was torn up on two fronts. He'd hired Toni, and she'd been so uncomfortable in the workplace *he* managed that she'd fled. Unacceptable. He'd also put Toni in this predicament by agreeing to be her date for the wedding. Also unacceptable. He'd failed at work and in his personal life. Toni knew how Denzin felt, and he didn't want to pressure her, especially not now. But he couldn't remain quiet. He needed to remind her that she wasn't alone. He pulled out his phone to send her a text.

> Denzin: I'm sorry, I should never have put you in this situation. How can I make it right?

His phone remained silent. No reply from Toni, not that he expected it immediately. She needed time and space.

Denzin turned to his computer and canceled his one-thirty, rebooking it for the next day—in person. He knew the yeti-friendly owner of Denali Powder. He'd make the drive to Denali for the meeting and stay a few days with Dale, giving Toni breathing room.

After settling his plans, Denzin returned home and packed. The mid-afternoon sun shone low on the horizon as he headed out. It would soon set since they were only a few weeks from solstice and the shortest, darkest day of the year. The dark usually didn't bother him, but today it added to the bleak feeling settling in his gut.

And as Wildwood disappeared in his rearview mirror, his mind and heart were still there with Toni. How was he ever going to make things right between them?

CHAPTER TWELVE

"I can't stay, Mari," Toni repeated, setting her phone on speaker as she haphazardly threw clothes into a suitcase.

"Slow down," Mari pleaded. "Let's talk this through. If you're uncomfortable at work, take a couple days off, then talk to Denzin."

Toni sputtered, her face likely turning purple. "I can't talk to Denzin. Don't you get that? I can't even complain to him that the new guy—who doesn't even know about yeti—thinks I'm being favored for screwing the boss because *Denzin is the boss*. This is why many businesses have rules against workplace romances. I should have known better."

"Wait, what new guy?"

"I mentioned him. Jeremy F-something. Fuckface?"

Mari huffed a dry laugh. "That's quite the last name."

"Whatever." In Toni's mind, he'd always be Fuckface, the inconsiderate asshole that found the chink in her very spotty armor. "I wanted to let you know that I'm going to Seattle to stay with my mom."

"For how long?"

Toni ran a hand through tangled hair. "I don't know. I bought a one-way ticket. I need to put some space between me and the mess I've gotten myself into. I need to be . . . not here. I don't have anywhere else to go."

"Oh, Toni." The pain in Mari's voice made her wince. "Please slow down. Think about this."

"I've done nothing but think. I need to get out of the situation. Wildwood doesn't feel . . ." She paused, searching for the right word. "Safe, stable. Not when Jeremy and others are questioning my professionalism. My mom might drive me bonkers, but I need something solid right now."

"Jeremy is the only person questioning you, Toni. He's an outlier."

"I dunno. Apparently, it was quite the topic at

the brewery last night. He even questioned how I received the grant."

Mari groaned. "Toni, it's him, not you. Please slow down. Besides, how are you going to explain Denzin to your mom?"

Toni let out a breath. "I don't know." She had nothing planned. It turned out that the ice wasn't only thin, it had been nonexistent, so she'd chucked the ice skates. Thankfully, she was prepared for any situation. With her proverbial running shoes back on and credit card in hand, she was ready to flee to higher ground where she might not be happy, but she'd feel less vulnerable.

"I booked the last seat on a redeye tonight."

"Tonight? Toni . . . no amount of my whining is going to stop you, is it? I'm tempted to block you in your driveway."

"I have a trail down to the road and a ride-sharing app on my phone." She looked down at the pile of clothes in her bag. Jeans, underwear, bras . . . no shirts.

While Mari rambled on about the reasons she shouldn't leave, Toni grabbed a couple of T-shirts and a fleecy Mountain High pullover. She paused, taking in the logo. Her softest, most comfortable sweatshirt reminded her of Denzin and thinking about him made her heart squeeze and her palms sweat. She rubbed at her chest and tossed it in anyway.

"Are you even listening to me, Toni?"

Toni picked up her phone and took it off speaker. "I gotta go, Mari. I need to leave a letter for Denzin at the office on my way to the airport. I'll be in touch."

She might have cut her friend off when she ended the call, but Toni was focused. Getting out of town wasn't the only decision she'd made tonight. She eyed the resignation letter on her table. She hated leaving Denzin short staffed, but it was the slow season. They'd get by. And she couldn't go on like this.

Toni zipped her suitcase, turned the thermostat down and all the lights off. Then she shoved her arms into her jacket and loaded her bag into her car.

The tears didn't start falling until she entered Denzin's office. They broke with a sob when his scent hit her. She might be torn up over a job she'd worked hard to earn, but at that moment she realized the actual pain lay in leaving Denzin.

DENZIN FLICKED on his high beams as he crossed over the railroad tracks and rounded the bend at the south end of Broad Pass. This time of day and year, traffic was sporadic, and his headlights were the only glow for miles.

He hadn't gone far before the truck's sound system alerted him to an incoming text. Normally he didn't turn it on, but he'd stayed connected, hoping to hear from Toni in places where he had cell coverage.

Mari's name flashed on the screen. He hit play, and a computerized voice read, "Call me. It's about Toni."

His heart lurched, and he pulled over at the next wide spot in the road to return the call.

As soon as she answered, Denzin demanded, "What's happened? Is Toni okay?"

"Physically, yes. Mentally, no. Zin, she's getting on a plane tonight for Seattle. She's freaking out, running."

Denzin swore under his breath. "Eddie asked about our relationship today during our staff meeting."

"It's not my place to say this, but you should know that the new guy accused her of sleeping with you to get her position at work and suggested she'd done the same to receive the grant."

Fuck! His fist came down on the steering wheel so hard it might have cracked. He'd known something was wrong before their meeting today. He'd never fired an employee, but Jeremy would be his first.

"I guess enough locals attended the wedding that someone apparently mentioned you two went together." Mari let out a long breath. "Zin, she left a letter for you."

This time his heart froze. "What kind of letter?" Why wouldn't she text him instead? Unless the letter . . .

"I don't know, but she left it at the office."

"Fuck," he snarled and swung the truck around. That sounded too much like a resignation letter, like she was backing out of their contract. Why else would she have left it at the office? "I'm an hour south of Denali but turning around, coming back. What time is her flight?"

"She didn't say, only that she'd booked a redeye tonight."

Denzin thanked Mari, ended the call, and pulled back onto the road. His truck flew over frost heaves in the pavement at speeds that made his iron stomach flip.

Even without traffic, it would take at least three and a half hours to get to the Anchorage airport. He didn't care about the risk of a yeti traveling into the city. He needed to stop Toni. If she would only talk to him, they could at least try to come up with a solution that would make her comfortable with her current employment. And they could work out a plan to deal with Jeremy and his slanderous lies—like run him out of town with torches and pitchforks.

If working together in the same office made Toni uncomfortable, Denzin could base himself out of the Palmer branch or work from home. They could arrange duties so she could keep her position, and they could interact less or not at all.

He punched a button on his steering wheel and verbally placed a call to Toni's phone. She didn't answer, but he left a message anyway. "Please don't leave, Toni. Let's talk things through. If you don't want to talk to me, you can relay your needs through Mari or someone else." He paused, then added. "I'm three hours from the airport, but I'm heading your way."

Denzin forced himself to slow to a reasonable speed. He might be willing to drive into the city, but the risk of a State Trooper pulling him over wasn't worth it. However, given the late hour, he made good time.

Once he arrived at the airport, he entered the long-term parking lot, circling the rows until he found Toni's car. He had no way of knowing how long ago she'd parked.

Of course, he couldn't storm into the airport. Yeti didn't have the luxury of going after humans in public places. He pulled out his phone.

> Denzin: I'm at the airport by your car. Please come out and talk to me.

He waited. A wave of people pulsed through the lot, scraped windshields, then drove off. Meanwhile, his phone remained silent, and Toni didn't appear. Eventually, he tapped one more message.

> Denzin: I'll stay for another twenty minutes.

To avoid suspicion, he pulled into a nearby parking spot. Time crept by. He stayed an additional thirty minutes before accepting defeat. At one in the morning, Denzin paid his parking fee at the automatic kiosk, then drove to the Mountain High building in Wildwood.

Dread pooled in his stomach as he made his way up the backstairs to his office. He froze outside the door. Toni's scent filled the hallway. As the sweet floral perfume of wild iris teased his senses, a fleeting burst of hope pulsed through him. Could she be inside, waiting for him?

Of course, she wasn't. Her car was parked at the airport. She'd come here to drop off a letter that he didn't want to read.

A single sheet of paper lay on his desk next to his keyboard. With a deep breath, Denzin picked it up.

The missive was short, to the point, and very formal. Toni had terminated her contract with Mountain High Guiding Service.

His thoughtless actions had caused a smart, talented professional to leave her job. And he couldn't help the profound feeling of personal rejection. By leaving without a word, Toni made it clear that she wasn't interested in pursuing a relationship with him. Unlike his breakup with Julia, his heart was most definitely involved this time. Like a thin sheet of ice, it had just shattered into a million pieces.

CHAPTER THIRTEEN

T oni stumbled, bleary-eyed, out of the rideshare and up to her mother's apartment. She'd slept fitfully in her cramped airplane middle seat on the three-hour overnight flight. It didn't help that a text from Denzin had come in just as they'd sealed the aircraft's door for departure.

Apparently opting for pain rather than blissful ignorance, she'd enabled free texting inflight. She received the next message from him once they were airborne. He'd chased after her, followed her to the airport, and waited by her car. By that point, she'd been gaining altitude over Prince William Sound. Anchorage and Wildwood were behind her.

Her heart, her entire chest, had become an empty cavern of pain.

Denzin hadn't texted again—she'd checked. Frequently. Not that Toni had responded to his texts. First, she needed to get to her mother's. Her mother's meddling had driven Toni into this mess, but right now staying with her felt more stable than being in Alaska. Once there, she'd figure out what to do.

"Antoinette!" her mother exclaimed when she opened the door, a fluttering hand rising to her neckline.

"I take it you didn't receive my message?"

"Message? On the phone?" She said this as if Toni would have communicated some other way. "I don't turn my phone on until the coffee is brewing, and I haven't even started a pot." She motioned for Toni to come in but looked past her, as if someone else might be with her. "Right, right. Of course, Denzin isn't with you."

Given Toni's lack of sleep, her overwrought emotions, and that she'd basically been running on adrenaline for hours, the mention of Denzin's name triggered a sob.

Her mother, dressed in her nightgown and robe, because it wasn't quite seven in the morning, pulled Toni into a hug. "Oh sweetheart. What's wrong? Is Denzin okay?"

Toni managed a nod.

"But things are not okay between you two?"

Another hiccup of tears burst out.

Her mother steered her toward the couch, helping her take off her jacket. "Sit down. I'll get the coffee going."

Toni, vision blurry from crying, grabbed a throw blanket and curled into a ball on the couch. The grinder whirred, and the smell of coffee wafted out of the small kitchen. Her tears slowed, and she shut her eyes as she waited for her mother to return.

The next thing Toni knew, she had a kink in her neck, and the throw she'd been leaning against was damp with drool. Gross. Her mother had covered her with another blanket. She pushed it back and stretched, glancing around to orient herself. The apartment no longer smelled like freshly ground beans, and it was quiet, too quiet.

"Mom?" Toni rose from the couch and padded into the kitchen. The clock on the microwave read one p.m. She'd been asleep for nearly six hours. Stifling a yawn, she returned to the living room. A slip of notebook paper on the table caught her eye.

Toni—You were sleeping so soundly I didn't want to disturb you. I have an appointment. Be back this evening. I made up the guest bed. XO—Mom

With some apprehension, Toni opened her phone to check her messages. Nothing from Denzin. Instead of the relief she expected, a profound sadness settled around her as she switched screens and scrolled through nearly a dozen messages from Mari. Toni replied that she'd safely arrived at her mother's.

Then she brushed her teeth, flossed—a new habit she'd picked up from Denzin—and crawled into the guest bed. She didn't care that it was the middle of the day. Exhaustion, both physical and emotional, overwhelmed her. Jeremy's accusations had triggered the urge to run and hide. Which is exactly what she did—run to her mom's and pull the covers over her head.

By the time she emerged early the next day, her stomach had turned itself inside out with hunger. She could hear her mother in the bathroom, so she got up, started the coffee, and put a piece of bread in the toaster.

"Well, you must be good and rested," her mother observed when she entered the kitchen several minutes later. "Feel better?"

"Only a little."

Her mother poured a cup of coffee and joined Toni at the table. "Did you and Denzin break up?"

Toni's heart sped, knowing she had to come clean. She swallowed her toast and took a sip from her mug. "About that. Mom, we were never in a relationship. We pretended to be in one so that you would stop trying to set me up with random men."

Her mother's cheeks colored. "Antoinette, if I—"

Toni held up a hand. "Creating an account on a dating site to find someone for me is way out of line. Mom, I need you to stop. Don't set me up on any more dates when I come to visit."

"Toni, I—"

"Will you promise? No more. I can date a million guys, but there is no guarantee that I'll find happiness with any of them. But do you know what made me happy? My job, my accomplishments, which you have never once acknowledged. Why can't you simply be proud of me and let me live my life?"

Her mother sputtered. "Of course I'm proud of you. You up and moved back to Alaska on your own and started a business. Your fourth-grade teacher reached out to say what an amazing job you're doing through outreach at Mountain High. All my friends down here are sick of hearing me brag about the grant you received, but I don't care. I'll boast about you to whoever will listen."

Toni sighed. "Why didn't you tell me that Mrs.

Scott reached out or that you're proud of me? Every time we talk, you ask about my social life and try to hook me up with another guy. It makes me feel like my accomplishments will never be enough for you if I'm single."

Pinching the bridge of her nose, her mother exhaled. "I don't want you to be alone, or lonely. I want you to have what your father and I had before he passed away—both the love and the security of a partner."

Toni reached for her mother's hand. "Maybe I'll have that one day, but you can't force it, and it's not up to you."

Her mother let out a gusty sigh and dabbed at her eyes. "At the risk of overstepping bounds, Antoinette, why are you here? And why are you referring to your job in the past tense?"

Toni slowly twirled her coffee cup. "I should not have pretended to have a relationship with Denzin—"

This time, her mother held up her hand. "Sweetheart, you can put any label on it you want, but there isn't anything fake about the affection you and Denzin hold for each other. You may have been trying to fool me, but perhaps you're fooling each other. Don't you like Denzin? He clearly cares for you."

Her mother logged into her phone, then passed it to Toni. "I knew as soon as I saw this picture that your regard for each other still ran deep. It always has."

A photo of Toni and Denzin filled the screen. His arms around her, eyes closed, and lips pressed to Toni's cheek. She looked surprised, but her wide smile betrayed her—that night at the Wildwood Brewery, she'd been thrilled by his kiss.

Tears welled in Toni's eyes. "Our relationship is making a Mountain High employee and others in town question the work I do and my role and effort in receiving the grant."

Her mother cupped her mug in both hands. "Is that what this is all about? Threats and gossip? Did your world fall apart when you went into work on Monday?"

Toni opened and closed her mouth. Her mother knew her too well.

"Did Denzin make you feel uncomfortable?"

Toni shook her head. "No. He's very conscientious and respectful of my feelings and boundaries." Her voice turned watery. "I want my personal and professional lives to remain separate. Mixing them together is complicated, stressful, and makes me uneasy. By deciding to go to the wedding with Denzin, as a fake couple or not, I inadvertently put all my eggs in one basket." She dropped her head to rest on her arm. "And now my basket's overturned, and my eggs are a broken, gooey mess. And Jeremy Fuckface is throwing them at me."

"Jeremy who?" Her mother tsked and shook her head. "Did you talk with Denzin about this? If he's as respectable as you say, he'd work with you to make it right and discredit any rumors."

"But *he's* part of the problem. The rumors will get worse if I run to him for help."

Her mother reached across the table and squeezed Toni's hand. "My advice is to be open and honest. Talk to Denzin. If you like him and want a relationship with him, pursue it. And if that desire conflicts with your business goals, then why not focus on your work with the city? You're the one getting the grant for the climbing wall—and you earned it, no matter what anyone else says. Why can't you manage the effort? Then your so-called eggs are in two baskets." She smiled before adding, "And you can chuck a few at this Jeremy fellow."

Toni huffed a laugh, then paused, her mind

whirring. For all her mother's matchmaking antics, she couldn't begrudge her this advice. She hadn't considered taking an active role with the rec center, instead thinking of herself as more of the invisible force behind the effort, not a hands-on manager. But she had management experience from previous jobs. "A job with the city might be possible. It wouldn't stop the rumors, though, even if baseless."

"There are always going to be people who crave gossip and drama. But if it makes you feel better about yourself and your situation, then pursue a job with the city." Her mother sipped her coffee then asked, "What did you say to Denzin before you left?"

"I-I didn't." An ache that had nothing to do with an empty stomach spread across Toni's middle. "I left a resignation letter on his desk and ignored his texts."

Her mother's face fell. "Then you hopped on a flight, leaving him no option to follow you. Yeti can't fly on a commercial jet. He couldn't even enter the airport."

"He did follow me," she admitted weakly. Tears stung again as she realized the enormity of her blind decision to run. "He waited for me in the parking lot, but I had already taken my seat on the plane."

"Sweetheart, I don't want to make things worse, but isn't that what Julia did to him?"

All the moisture in Toni's mouth evaporated. "But I . . ." Her heart hammered as a sickening realization dawned. Oh god. What had she done? She'd been so focused on her own life, her own discomfort, that she'd never stopped to consider Denzin's position. The only difference between herself and Julia? Julia had already been with his brother when she left town.

Toni stood, a frantic feeling clawing at her. Why had she been so quick to leave? Why hadn't she listened to Mari, or womanned up and confided her fears to Denzin? "I need to go home. Now. To Wildwood. To Denzin."

DENZIN CALLED in all his favors Tuesday morning to keep Mountain High open without Toni. While Eddie covered the school groups, Denzin terminated Jeremy and arranged for his final paycheck. They had plenty of reasons to let the new guy go.

But as Wednesday dawned, Denzin's options were limited. Eddie had commitments at the Palmer office, and he'd already made the long drive between Palmer and Wildwood two days in a row.

They operated with a skeleton crew in winter, and yeti like Denzin, Pema, and Dorje couldn't support in-person customer service. While Mari had the skills to run the storefront, she had a full-time job in the kitchen at the retirement center. They had other human staff located in Palmer, but Denzin didn't want to ask any of them to make the extended commute. Plus, some of them didn't know that yeti existed—which is why Pema worked evenings in Palmer.

He couldn't sleep, so he drove to the office early to hang a "closed for the week" sign on the front door of the Mountain High building. As soon as the local school opened, he called to postpone the scheduled groups. When they asked after Toni, he told them she was unavailable. He didn't want to say more, not now. It would feel too depressingly real and permanent to tell them she'd resigned.

He'd given himself the week to consider how to respond—or not—to her letter. Technically, it didn't need a response. She'd ended their contract. But if she changed her mind and was open to discussion, they could determine a new path forward, like shifting who she reported to.

Fuck, the way he felt today, he'd be ready to resign and give her *his* position. A human would be better suited for his job anyway. Being furry under his office slacks and collared shirts meant he couldn't even train a new employee unless they knew about yeti—the reason Toni had taken on Jeremy's training.

What value did Denzin bring to Mountain High Guiding Service? Sure, he could make a deal in writing or over the phone, but if the task required his face, he couldn't do it. After this week, the owners might realize that he'd become a liability, not an asset.

He sat in his big office, the rest of the building empty and shuttered, effectively unable to do his job. And the woman he cared about most in the world had left him. His self-worth had hit rock bottom. Again.

Denzin released his stress ball. It didn't roll across his desk, now a misshapen egg, not quite able to regain its original spherical shape after the workout he'd given it.

He followed up on some correspondence and new business opportunities, but his heart wasn't in it —likely because, for the first time in his life, it was broken. Eventually, he dragged himself home.

His house felt especially hollow and empty that

afternoon. Denzin changed out of his work clothes, tossed his phone on his dresser, and shrugged into his outdoor gear. With no destination in mind, he left out the back door and began climbing toward the peaks beyond, unsure if he wanted to lose or find himself in the Chugach Mountains.

CHAPTER FOURTEEN

O f course there were headwinds during Toni's return trip to Anchorage. The pilot had the nerve to chuckle when he announced that the estimated flight time would be four hours. Usually, the travel time took closer to three, sometimes under. Toni wanted to jump out of the plane and push it, make it go faster.

Before she'd left her mother's, she'd sent a text to Denzin, telling him she wanted to talk if he was still willing. She'd texted again to give him her flight number and arrival time. She'd also messaged to apologize but explained that she needed to give her full apology in person.

Her phone remained silent.

What did that mean? Had Denzin grown tired of

her? He didn't play games, but now she knew how he felt when she hadn't responded. She didn't deserve any better.

The plane landed at ten p.m., thirty minutes late. Toni hustled through the airport with her carry-on suitcase and out to her frosty car. The ice on her windshield and windows proved to be the stubborn kind that took extra muscle to scrape off. Finally, with a clear line of sight and a warm engine, she hit the highway and raced back to Wildwood.

Since she now knew exactly how to get to Denzin's, she roared through the snowy mountainside roads at speeds entirely too fast for conditions. Her dash clock read eleven when she came to a halt outside his log house. The plowed driveway didn't hold any vehicles. Had he parked in the garage, or was he away from home?

Her car had triggered a motion detector light, but the house otherwise sat dark and silent. Toni rushed past the unlit ice lanterns and up the walk to the front door. She half expected Denzin to meet her there, having heard her car roar up and seeing the light. But the door was closed, so she knocked.

Getting no answer, she hunted for a doorbell. While the motion-triggered lights flooded the driveway, the front door remained in shadow. She didn't see a doorbell—her cell phone did little to help—so she knocked again. When the house remained silent, she sent Denzin another text. Maybe he hadn't heard her car but would hear a notification from his phone.

The winter cold seeped in as she stood and waited. Her shoes squeaked on dry snow when she bounced from foot to foot to stay warm. The motion detector light turned off, plunging Toni into complete darkness—except for the million stars overhead. It would have been brilliant *if* Denzin had been with her.

Where could he be? Or did he choose not to answer? A quiet desperation ate away at Toni. She eyed the door then tried the handle. It opened. But was that good or bad? If Denzin lay fast asleep in his bed, she didn't want to startle him. She ran her hand along the wall in the entry hall until she found a light switch. She flipped it on and called out, "Denzin? It's Toni."

The house remained silent, but she tentatively forged ahead. She flicked on lights as she slipped from room to room, calling out like one might do for a bear when hiking on an overgrown trail in summer.

Denzin's truck filled the garage, she'd entered the room from inside the house, but he wasn't home. Toni turned off most of the lights and perched on the couch to wait for him, having no idea if this was normal or if she should file a missing person—er, yeti —report.

She dozed off—she had to stop making a habit of falling asleep on other people's couches—when a noise from the back of the house made her bolt upright. The hair on her arms stood on end as she strained to identify what had woken her.

She opened her mouth to call out again, but the hall light extinguished, and she swallowed her words as jitters got the better of her. She'd broken into Denzin's house and napped on his couch without him knowing it.

"Hello?" she called, her voice sounding weak and raspy.

A loud, demanding voice, nothing like Denzin's, boomed, "Who's there?"

Toni nearly pissed her pants but had enough presence of mind to identify herself, for better or worse. "Toni. It's Toni." She sounded like herself this time.

The light came on, and Denzin stepped around the corner as he pulled back the hood to his jacket. "Toni? What are you doing here?"

"Hi, uh, I found the door unlocked and . . . did you get my texts?"

He blinked, then shook his head, looking slightly bewildered. "I haven't had my phone on me."

She let out a breath she didn't know she'd been holding and squeezed her eyes shut. "Denzin, I owe you an apology." Such an understatement.

TONI STOOD in the middle of his living room. Denzin considered pinching himself. Hopefully, he hadn't fallen asleep in the snow only to dream this whole scenario. It would suck if he woke up alone in a snowbank. If this was a hallucination, it was damn convincing. He realized now that her scent filled the room. It curled around him like warm, caressing fingers.

However, her apology, just like her sudden presence, caught him off guard. Her name came out as a hoarse whisper. She'd returned and come to his house in the middle of the night.

But what did it mean?

"I'm sorry," Toni continued, her hands clenching tightly at her sides. "I got scared, and I shut you out. I ran. I acted cowardly and selfish." She closed her eyes for a moment, a pained look on her face that he wanted to erase.

"Really selfish," she emphasized. "So focused on how uncomfortable *I* was that I didn't take your feelings or the consequences of my actions into account. I didn't give you the respect you deserve. I hope you can forgive me."

Denzin took in a measured breath, fighting a quick response of, "It's okay." He wasn't okay. And maybe she'd only sought him out to clear her conscience. He chose his words carefully, trying not to leave himself in a more vulnerable position. Because what he really wanted to do was scoop Toni into his arms and never let go—but she might not have come here for that. Dating a yeti wasn't easy for a human. He had to respect that he'd not only asked Toni to give *him* a chance, but the yeti lifestyle and all its limitations. "I appreciate the apology," he said, then added, "Everyone will be glad you've returned."

The shadows under her eyes turned darker. "Everyone?" she echoed, her voice sounding hollow. "Not you?"

The ache in his chest grew, and he quietly admitted, "You already know how I feel. That hasn't changed."

She took a step closer, her gaze locked on his and Denzin's breathing became erratic. "Thank you for being brave enough to share your feelings with me during the party, Denzin. I should have told you then, I like you, too. I have since high school. You must have overheard my mother confirm as much the other night. It's true." A rosy blush colored her cheeks, but she didn't look away. "You were my first kiss, and the crush I've never gotten over."

Her declaration, while welcome, wasn't a surprise. But it still didn't speak to the future.

Toni continued. "When I took the job with Mountain High, it thrilled me to both work for the company and with you, but it also meant I've had to tamp down my crush. However, as much as I tried to convince myself that I'd meet someone else, that my feelings would change, they haven't. It's always been you, even when you were my off-limits boss."

Denzin's breath caught. This was torture.

"Under the pretense of a fake relationship, I gave myself permission to explore my affection for you, my urges, desires. I allowed myself to ignore my fear and the part of me that believed I shouldn't be dating my employer. I went for it." She gave him a shy smile. "I think we both did."

His fingers flexed, wanting to reach for her, and he took a small step narrowing the gap between them.

"I knew that having a romantic relationship with

you could complicate things at work. However, I underappreciated how unbalanced I'd feel when we stopped pretending, and I wasn't truly prepared for anyone to call me out on it."

A low growl rumbled from Denzin's chest. "I fired Jeremy." He held up a hand when Toni's eyes went wide. "I didn't do it in retaliation but because of his actions. He had several marks against him prior to his inappropriate comments to you. He could have brought his concerns about our relationship to Eddie, a manager, or the company owners, rather than make spiteful remarks."

She offered a weak smile. "I should have brought it to your attention right away." Her smile turned into a grimace. "And about me leaving . . . I realize that there are a lot of similarities between how I acted and how Julia left you."

Denzin grunted. The reminder of being dumped was like a punch to his already sore gut. "She left with my brother."

"She dumped you, your limited lifestyle, then left Alaska. Went somewhere you could never go. She left you behind. And by running off to my mother's, I did the same thing. I'm so sorry about that."

"You and Julia are nothing alike."

"I do want to make one clear distinction. Julia

came to Alaska for adventure." Toni's throat worked as she swallowed, her eyes glistening. "I returned to Alaska last year because it's my home but also because of you, Denzin."

His heart thundered, and he allowed himself to hope as she continued, "I came here tonight to apologize, to share my feelings with you, and to figure out a solution that will work for both of us. I love my job at Mountain High, but . . ."

"I don't want you to quit," Denzin blurted. "You shouldn't have to. We can rewrite your contract so you don't report to me. And if that's not a workable solution, *I'll* resign—no strings attached. That might be better anyway."

Her eyes narrowed. "Denzin, no. You can't leave Mountain High. It's grown so much under your leadership. The company wouldn't be what it is now without you." She shook her head. "No."

But he didn't want to be the reason for her departure. "You're more important than any job, regardless of what happens between us. I will take full responsibility for the choices I made, even if that means quitting."

A slow, shy smile spread across her face. "Thank you for that offer, but here's my proposal. I would like to reinstate my contract, but only temporarily, until we find and train a replacement."

His pulse whooshed in his ears. Professional or personal, he didn't want temporary with Toni.

"I reached out to the city today and reread the terms of the grant. I'm applying to manage the new climbing wall at the rec center. I love working at Mountain High and with you. But I'd also love managing the climbing wall. And given the choice between having a great job or having a great job plus the option of dating you . . ." She peered up at him. "For real this time," she clarified. "I'd choose the option that came with you."

Denzin blinked. Did Toni mean what he thought she meant? Was she really choosing *him*?

She took a step closer. "Will you forgive me, Denzin? Can we give *us* a try?"

"I can't take you to France," he said.

Toni laughed. "Not a priority for me."

"I can't take you to dinner."

Toni inched closer. "I like eating in."

"I—" he began, but Toni cut him off.

"Denzin, I want you. The leader. The boss. The yeti. I want the whole package. What do you say? Will you forgive me?"

He exhaled a ragged breath. *Fuck. Yes!* Denzin closed the space between himself and Toni and crushed her to his body. "Of course I forgive you. But the blame isn't all yours. In my position, I should never have agreed to a fake relationship. I acted selfishly, too." He scooped her up, lifting her until her face was level with his. Toni wrapped her legs around him, squeezing his body and his heart. "I wanted—still want—you, regardless of the consequences," he added, his voice low, husky. "Yes, I want to give *us* a try."

Toni's hungry mouth descended on his. The sweet press of her lips and the eager swipe of her tongue triggered a deep rumble in his chest. *Mine.* "I'm taking you to bed, Toni. If you don't want to go, jump down."

She tightened her legs, and her teeth grazed his earlobe. "I want you, Denzin. I want the slow lovemaking you promised at the cabin."

But as he began to carry her to his bedroom, she arched away from him. "My purse." She gestured toward a small, dark bag on the couch. Denzin moved toward it, and she grabbed the strap and slid it over her shoulder.

Her warm, brown eyes danced with mischief. "I have two condoms in here. I think they're your size."

He rested his forehead against hers. "I have a

confession to make. I took all the condoms from the cabin. I'd hoped we'd want them."

Toni's giggle delighted him. "Too bad we have work in the morning."

"We don't, actually. I closed the office for the rest of the week. I didn't have any employees to run it."

Toni sucked air between her teeth. "Sorry. But I'm not sorry if that means we get to stay in bed all day tomorrow."

"The rest of the week," Denzin amended.

A cute blush spread across Toni's cheeks before she grew serious again. "Since we're confessing . . . what I said earlier is true. I've had feelings for you since we were teenagers. Those feelings have grown stronger over this past year." She swallowed, her eyes locked with his. "And I think the last few days were so hard because . . . well, because I'm already in love with you, Denzin."

Denzin stared into Toni's soft brown eyes. He'd longed to hear those words from her. "Say it again?" he rasped, his voice raw with emotion and a vulnerability he rarely showed.

She cocked her head, her lips curving into a warm smile. "I love you," she said before kissing him tenderly.

Heat flushed through his body. When had he last

heard the word love directed toward him? Not since his mother had died. And he knew without a doubt he felt the same for Toni. It wouldn't have hurt so badly when she left if he didn't.

Denzin growled and tightened his grip. "I love you, too, Antoinette."

"Take me to bed," she breathlessly pleaded.

He pressed a kiss to her already swollen lips. "With pleasure."

CHAPTER FIFTEEN

The next morning Toni knew exactly where she was when she woke up—on top of Denzin. There was nowhere else she'd rather be than with him, in his bed, his space, his juniper and sandalwood scent curling around her body like a second skin.

They hadn't closed the bedroom curtains, the stars too beautiful to miss, though most of their focus had been on each other all night. A faint glow on the horizon hinted at an approaching winter dawn, but brilliant dots of light lingered in the sky.

Denzin's hard body and teasing fur caressed Toni's bare skin. She brushed a hand across his chest, a solid expanse of muscle, while his fingers whispered along her shoulder blades.

"Good morning, Toni." His deep voice was gentle, caring. "Sleep well?"

Last time they'd woken up together, she'd lied and said everything was fine when inside, she'd been freaking out.

At her pause, his hand stilled. "If you're having any doubts, please tell me."

This morning, she felt calm, at peace. She lifted her head to meet his gaze. "I'm indescribably happy. I know I made the right choice by returning home to you. This is where I belong." She pushed up to cradle his face. "I love you, Denzin. And now that we're together, I know everything else will fall into place."

DENZIN WOULD NEVER tire of hearing those three little words from Toni. Never. He opened his mouth to tell her he loved her as well, but she pressed a finger to his lips.

"I'm not done," she explained with a coy smile. "You amaze me. You face countless challenges every day, living as a yeti in a human-dominated world. And yet, you always excel. You're a tremendous asset to Mountain High and the Wildwood community—

even if most of them will never know how sexy you look in a suit."

Denzin huffed a laugh while his face heated at her praise. She made him feel valuable, like he was worth something after all. "I love you, too, Toni." He brushed a strand of hair from her face. "I'm so glad you're home." He felt complete with Toni back in Wildwood, back in his arms.

He thought of all the times he'd surreptitiously watched her lithe body flow across the bouldering wall. Those muscular thighs were smooth under his palms. He cupped her soft hips and tugged her toward him before leaning forward and pressing his lips to hers, then brushing light kisses across her cheek to her ear.

He whispered, "Do you know what I find sexy? How driven you are. Seeing all you accomplished with the city was a huge turn-on."

Her laugh burst out, eyes twinkling. "What if someone else did it?"

"Then it would only be impressive," he said with a wink.

His cock stirred as her long, bare legs clenched around him. He lightly stroked the curve of her hips and the backs of her thighs.

She quirked an eyebrow at his touch, then leaned

in to nibble his earlobe, her teeth scraping his skin. Denzin gave an involuntary shudder, and she laughed. "I thought so," she said with an air of triumph. "I'm learning you."

She brushed her mouth against his before tracing his lips with her finger "I also love these. Celestial blue—that's how I'd describe the color of your lips. Like the sky on a perfect winter day. They're full, lush, and give the most sumptuous kisses."

"You bring out the best in my lips," he growled, lightly catching her finger between his teeth and sucking it in, swirling his tongue around it.

Toni groaned, eyelids lowering as she pulled her finger from his mouth. "I also love your textured tongue, especially when it's anywhere on my body."

He chuckled. "Noted."

Her hand fluttered along the side of his face as she continued her cataloging. "I love your eyes. Sometimes they look positively stormy, and I want to calm them."

She pressed forward, the bare mounds of her breasts flattening against his chest as she slowly rocked back and forth. "I've fantasized about rubbing my naked body against your fur. And it's every bit as thrilling as I knew it would be."

With a groan, Denzin slid Toni down his torso

until the head of his now erect cock bumped against her.

Her eyes lit, and she pointedly glanced at the roll of condoms on his nightstand. "I think I'm about to go for a ride."

"Mmmm . . . I hope so," he rumbled.

His brother's discarded wedding invitation lay beneath the condoms. A week ago, Denzin had resented that wedding. Now he was glad for it.

He'd gone from feeling lonely and unworthy to having Toni in his bed professing her love. What more could he ask for?

"I love so many things about you, too, Toni. And I want to show you, again and again."

Her lips slid into a sultry smile. "Oh, I'm game."

He couldn't stop the growl that formed deep in his chest. "Good," he said before covering her lips with his. And then he showed her how much he loved her. Again and again.

EPILOGUE

New Year's Eve

The clock above the large fireplace at Toklat Lodge read five minutes to midnight. Rabten and Helen shared caretaker duties for the remote luxury destination this winter while it was closed to the public and cut off from the road system during the snowy months. The limited fly-in access made it a perfect New Year's Eve party location for a large group of yeti and their friends.

As Denzin scanned the room for Toni, a pair of bare arms snaked around him from behind, sliding under his tuxedo jacket and encircling his middle. At Toni's coaxing, they'd both donned their formal wear for the evening. Turns out he had a reason to wear his tux again.

"Looking for someone in particular?"

His lips quirked at Toni's game. "I am. She's the world to me. Brunette, about so tall." He raised his hand to shoulder height.

Toni circled Denzin, his arm wrapping around her as she leaned into him.

Denzin splayed his hand across her hip, drawing her closer.

Toni beamed up at him. "Thank you for hosting me and my mom at your house for solstice and Christmas. She enjoys spending time with us." Toni slid her arms up to his shoulders and began swaying to the jazz mix that Tseten had selected. "I'm glad you were able to reschedule your trip to Denali."

"About those plans. They were very tentative."

Her eyes narrowed. "I checked your schedule."

He grinned down at her. "Of course I had it on my calendar. I had a diligent contractor that would undoubtedly check for it."

"I had a hunch you'd planned that trip on the fly," she admitted, snickering. "And I'm still your diligent contractor until we find a replacement. The city said my start date could be flexible."

Denzin twirled Toni, her deep red dress shimmering in the glow of twinkle lights. When she came back into his arms, he said, "You realize that I've gotten the best deal out of having you and your mother stay with me?" He lowered his head, his mouth at her ear, and whispered, "I've woken up with you in my arms each morning. No returning to your cabin."

Her eyes gleamed in response. "On that note, my mother brought up a good point at Thanksgiving. It might make financial sense to, you know . . ."

"Carpool to work?" he teased.

She smirked in response. "I like waking up with you too, Denzin. I want to every morning. What if I move in with you? I'd ask you to move in with me, but that makes no sense since you're the one with the big house. If it's too soon, I understand. It's just that—"

Denzin's chest tightened. He'd wanted this but hadn't wanted to rush Toni. "Yes," he said, cutting her off as he tightened his arms around her, his body thrumming with the rightness of making a life with Toni. "Yes, I want you to move in. Yes, I want you in my bed every night. Yes, I want to share my home with you. And carpool," he added with a grin. "I've also thought about it. A lot. But then, I think about you a lot."

A countdown to midnight began across the room.

Toni's wide smile made his heart sing. "So, we're moving in together?"

"As soon as we're back in Wildwood. Now, should we give this crowd a kiss they'll be talking about for years to come?"

"We owe it to them," she said, then added with a wink, "and ourselves."

Not to disappoint the crowd, or his no-longer-fake girlfriend, Denzin would make this kiss another that neither he nor Toni would ever forget.

He lowered his face to hers. "Happy kissiversary, Toni."

Her lips smiled against his as she let out a soft laugh. "Happy kissiversary, Denzin."

Thank you for reading Fake Dating Her Yeti! Please consider leaving a review. Reviews make it easier for others to find this book.

Want to see what happens at the office when Denzin is no longer Toni's boss? For a FREE BONUS SCENE visit www.nevapostauthor.com/fake-datingheryeti-bonus

Love ya some yeti? Check out Gina and Dorje's story in Yeti for Love.

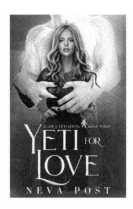

A yeti ice climbing instructor who's too hot for his harness.

In search of a new adventure, Gina moves to the frosty wilds of Alaska. She never expected to fall helmet over crampons for Dorje—*a yeti*—whose hotness could melt a glacier. He possesses mad climbing skills, a penchant for baking, and the ability to sweep her off her feet. In Dorje, Gina realizes she's found her ultimate adventure.

A free spirit who sparkles like fresh snow.

Dorje copes with recent loss by knitting and binging telenovelas. As his yarn budget dwindles, he reluctantly returns to work, teaching charismatic newbie Gina to ice climb. When he accidentally reveals his yeti secret, she doesn't scream and run. She invites him to dinner. Gina is strong, confident and brings the first smile to his face in over a year.

Gina can now conquer a frozen waterfall, but can she scale the walls around Dorje's heart and convince him that life is better when they're roped together?

SNEAK PEEK OF YETI FOR LOVE

Dorje was watching the mountain goats, but Gina was watching him.

She shifted in his lap to see his face better. When he'd picked her up like she was no heavier than a box of bubble wrap and whisked her under the ledge, the neck gator he used as a mask had fallen.

A trimmed, snowy-white beard lined a pronounced jaw, and whiskers prickled her palm when she cupped his cheek. His beard framed full lips the color of deep-blue, winter twilight. They were lush. Kissable. Her gaze lingered as her fingertips explored.

Dorje's growl reverberated through her body, the sensation pooling between her thighs. Possibly because they were spread wide to straddle one of his enormous legs. Her core throbbed in response.

"It's not a skin condition," he said, his voice hushed and raspy.

Her hands moved to his goggles. "I want to see you." But she didn't remove them, wouldn't if he didn't want her to. "Please."

His hands covered hers. Gone were the giant black gloves. In their place were warm, blue fingers and white hair on his wrists that ghosted over her skin like a soft downy feather. She fought a shiver at the pleasurable sensation. Then he slowly helped her lift the goggles.

He whispered her name like a plea and a confession.

Gina took him in, continuing to explore with her eyes and hands.

Azure lips contrasted with lighter blue skin. It reminded her of the depths of the ice cave. His trim white beard led to longer, softer, white . . . fur? She swallowed. Yes, fur—along the side of his face, his head. She lightly rubbed at his temples where it had matted under his goggles.

Eyes the color of an aquamarine gemstone stole her breath. The goats could have stampeded through the creek bed, and still she couldn't have torn her gaze away. Her smile grew. Then she giggled. "Dorje, you have some seriously big secrets, don't you?" She paused, then asked, "What are you?"

His chest rose and fell with a sigh. "A yeti."

"That's so badass."

"We, ah, need to talk."

"I'll say."

Order your copy today!

ALSO BY NEVA POST

Alaska Yeti Series:

Ready for Her Yeti

Fake Dating Her Yeti

Yeti for Love

$\sim$ *Coming soon* $\sim$

Rescued by Her Yeti

Married to Her Yeti

Loved by Her Yeti

ACKNOWLEDGMENTS

A huge thank you to Elizabeth, Erin, Heather, Karen, and Kristin. I wouldn't have made it this far without your input and encouragement.

A heartfelt thank you to Scott and all my family for their continued support.

ABOUT THE AUTHOR

Neva Post grew up in a log house in Interior Alaska where she walked uphill both ways to school at temperatures of negative forty with only the aurora borealis to light her way. At least, that's how she remembers it.

She's equally happy on a snowy trail or coaxing vegetables to grow in her garden during the long Alaskan summer days. When she's not waxing skis or chasing voles out of her cabbage, she's at her computer. Neva's novels include paranormal elements—she can't help it—with smart and dependable characters who always get their HEA.

www.nevapostauthor.com

facebook.com/nevapostauthor

instagram.com/nevapostauthor

Made in the USA
Columbia, SC
16 September 2024

41476690R00136